MAFIA TIES

AN ITALIAN CARTEL SEQUEL

SHANDI BOYES

D1367115

Edited by CAROLYN WALLACE

Illustrated by SSB COVERS & DESIGN

Edited by MIRYAM DENNY-IPENBURG

COPYRIGHT

Cover: SSB Covers and Design

Editing: Carolyn Wallace

Proofing: Miryam Denny-Ipenburg

Cover Image: Depositphotos

DEDICATION

To those brave enough not to pick.

I can't choose between them either.

Shandi xx

WANT TO STAY IN TOUCH?

Facebook: facebook.com/authorshandi

Instagram: instagram.com/authorshandi

Email: authorshandi@gmail.com

Reader's Group: bit.ly/ShandiBookBabes

Website: authorshandi.com

Newsletter: subscribepage.com/AuthorShandi

Play List

Wishing Well — Juice WRLD

Mood Swings — Pop Smole, Lil TJay

Such a Whore — JVLA

Sorry - Halsey

The Sound of Silence — Disturbed

The Night We Met — Gavin Mikhail

ALSO BY SHANDI BOYES

Perception Series

Saving Noah (Noah & Emily)

Fighting Jacob (Jacob & Lola)

Taming Nick (Nick & Jenni)

Redeeming Slater (Slater and Kylie)

Saving Emily (Noah & Emily - Novella)

Wrapped Up with Rise Up (Perception Novella - should be read after the Bound Series)

Enigma

Enigma (Isaac & Isabelle #1)

Unraveling an Enigma (Isaac & Isabelle #2)

Enigma The Mystery Unmasked (Isaac & Isabelle #3)

Enigma: The Final Chapter (Isaac & Isabelle #4)

Beneath The Secrets (Hugo & Ava #1)

Beneath The Sheets(Hugo & Ava #2)

Spy Thy Neighbor (Hunter & Paige)

The Opposite Effect (Brax & Clara)

I Married a Mob Boss(Rico & Blaire)

Second Shot(Hawke & Gemma)

The Way We Are(Ryan & Savannah #1)

The Way We Were(Ryan & Savannah #2)

Sugar and Spice (Cormack & Harlow)

Lady In Waiting (Regan & Alex #1)

Man in Queue (Regan & Alex #2)

Couple on Hold(Regan & Alex #3)

Enigma: The Wedding (Isaac and Isabelle)

Silent Vigilante (Brandon and Melody #1)

Hushed Guardian (Brandon & Melody #2)

Quiet Protector (Brandon & Melody #3)

Bound Series

Chains (Marcus & Cleo #1)

Links(Marcus & Cleo #2)

Bound(Marcus & Cleo #3)

Restrain(Marcus & Cleo #4)

Psycho (Dexter & ??)

Russian Mob Chronicles

Nikolai: A Mafia Prince Romance (Nikolai & Justine #1)

Nikolai: Taking Back What's Mine (Nikolai & Justine #2)

Nikolai: What's Left of Me(Nikolai & Justine #3)

Nikolai: Mine to Protect(Nikolai & Justine #4)

Asher: My Russian Revenge (Asher & Zariah)

I won the battle.
I massacred my enemies and freed my daughter from captivity.
My family is safe, but what happens when the woman I love
believes family ties go way deeper than direct descendants?

His veins hold my father's blood.
Some may say he is the true heir of the Petretti entity.
But he isn't without his weaknesses.

His castle will be stormed no matter what.
I just need to decide which side of the moat I will be on.
Family comes first of all—they just fail to mention what should
happen when your brother is also your enemy.

Mafia Ties is a ten-chapter sequel of Dimitri and Roxanne's
story. It jumps years into the future to show the events
surrounding Nikolai's arrival to Hopeton minus an invitation
and with no plans to unify ties between brothers.

**Also includes a bonus extended chapter solely in Nikolai's*
*POV ***

Mafia Ties

Dimitri & Roxanne

Four perfectly smitten years later...

1

DIMITRI

With my ass braced on the vanity sink, and my eyes locked on a white stick I'm praying like fuck will turn a shade of blue, I fold my arms in front of my chest. Roxanne is adamant I'm wrong. She is convinced pricks like Dr. Klein know her body more intimately than me.

Dr. Klein learned the hard way what happens when you hurt those I love. Tonight, I'll add a heap of conviction to the belief I'd go to the end of the earth to protect my family. Whether snuggled in their beds like Fien and Matteo are now or growing in my wife's womb, like I'm confident my next kid is, I will protect my family no matter what because family comes first of all.

They are *all* I live for.

Money, drugs, and power mean nothing to me anymore. Don't get me wrong, all the above-mentioned are a part of my industry, they also ensure my family will never want for anything, they're just no longer responsible for the circulation of my blood anymore. That honor belongs solely to Roxanne and our children.

When Roxanne was fighting for her life, I pledged that my girls would want for nothing. I've kept my promise. Unlike my father, I cherish my family.

I fight *for* them.

I work hard *for* them.

And I slice out the tongue of any stupid fuck who dares to sneer their last name in vain *for* them.

My wife and children give the Petretti name valor, and I won't have an insolent prick tell them any different. If you can't say my family name without a hint of pride behind it, it'll do you best to keep your mouth shut. That's the only guarantee you'll make it out of our exchange alive. You don't have to like the things my father did, you don't have to agree with how I run my businesses, but you sure as hell better respect me and my family or it will cost you more than your life.

My half smirk that makes Roxanne's head get into a tizzy years after seeing it for the first time drops half an inch when a shocked grumble escapes Roxanne's lips. She's staring at the pregnancy test Rosa purchased for her at my request, wide-eyed and open-mouthed. It turned blue like I was hoping, and although I'm not overly familiar with pregnancies since Matteo was born a little over three years ago, I know what those blue lines mean. I did good, and for the first time in a long time, it's taking everything I have not to shout it from the rooftops.

Can you blame me? Dr. Klein's disclosure when he strived to discount Roxanne's claims she was ever pregnant exposed she had a severe case of polycystic ovary syndrome. As far as he, and many other professionals since then have stated, Roxanne shouldn't have fallen pregnant with Matteo as easily as she did. It should have been a long drawn out process like the past three years have been.

I wasn't lying when I told Roxanne I'd have her knocked up with my kid the instant the trap I snared her with loosened its grip of her ankle. I killed her boyfriend, tortured her parents, and had threatened to kill her more times than I told her I loved her. I couldn't risk the sheen on my bastard exterior fading enough she'd see the real me.

I'd rather steal the light from her eyes than ever see her with another man, and since there's no fucking chance I'd ever do that, I had no choice but to keep the spark well-lit. Knocking her up with my kid again seemed like the next logical step.

She was already the perfect mother to Fien, but she knocked it out of the fucking park when Matteo was born. My woman is so strong, she birthed my child without drugs, at home, all because she knew of my wish to keep Matteo and Fien off my enemies' radars.

I'd be lying if I said the strength of my woman doesn't thicken my cock with adrenaline. I'm a cold-blooded killer, but even someone as hard as me can admit he has a soft spot for his woman.

Roxanne's inclusion in my life hasn't just kept my dick the most satisfied it's ever been, she has also made me a better man, which in turn also made me a better father. For that alone, I owe her more than any amount my bank accounts will ever hold.

Lucky for me, possessions aren't something Roxanne craves.

Possessiveness... that's an entirely different story.

Just like I'll never be a gentleman, my woman will never be a lady, but I wouldn't want her any other way.

"What did I tell you, Roxanne? Your cunt is sweeter when you're knocked up."

She shivers when I step closer to her, eager to authenticate my claim. Our mid-morning fuck when she got hot and bothered watching me command our realm commenced my campaign to prove two and a half years of nonstop fucking finally produced more than nail marks down my back, but that hard and fast fuck on my desk was hours ago and I'm nothing close to being patient.

"And I'm about ready for a second helping of dessert."

The positive pregnancy test, along with a heap of Roxanne's cosmetics, fall to the floor with a clatter when I swipe my arm across the gleaming marble material. The scent I've snorted more eagerly than I did coke in my youth hardens my cock when I plant Roxanne's backside onto the counter between the sinks of our master bathroom. I don't need to touch her panties to know they're drenched through. I can smell how aroused she is.

"Wider," I say on a growl when she spreads her thighs wide enough my hand can slip between her legs, but nowhere near extensive enough I can drag my tongue up the slit of her greedy cunt. I'm starved of her taste, and I'm not a man who holds back on his drug of choice.

"Keep them there."

After spreading her knees so far apart, her scant panties can be seen from the main part of our bedroom, I move for the door.

I'm not just closing it so Smith's perverted-fucking-self doesn't get off hearing the moans of my wife, I'm hoping it will reduce the chance Roxanne's shouts will wake Matteo.

Fien is so accustomed to the noises that rock out of the room I share with Roxanne every night she thinks they're normal. Matteo still struggles with the belief he needs to protect his mother when she's screaming like she is being murdered.

That's my fault.

I raised him with the morals my father forgot to instill in me.

He won't ever raise his hand to a woman, but he sure as fuck will when it comes to defending her. He only turned three two months ago, however, he had no issue putting a bully double his age and size on his ass at the playground last week when he pushed a little girl off the swing.

That punk-ass weasel should consider himself lucky. If he had treated Fien as he did the girl on the swing next to her, Matteo would have choked him out with the swing chains. That's how fearless he is when it comes to protecting those he loves. He's as ruthless and unhinged as his father.

I would have suggested he cool it a little if I hadn't seen the gaga eyes his rescuee was giving him. She was smitten with him just as quickly as I was when I spotted Roxanne with black smears under her eyes and chunky, Goth-approved boots. It reminded me that not every story needs a hero. Sometimes the villain gets a lead role as well.

As I pace back to Roxanne's side of the bathroom, I remove my belt from my trousers. Unlike the time where my anger got the better of me, she doesn't tremble in fear that I'm going to beat her with it.

I've studied every inch of her body the past almost four years. I know every pore, every goosebump, and every imperfect flaw, so I'm more than aware the widening of her pupils now has nothing to do with fear. She's turned on at the idea of being dominated, and I'm more than capable of fulfilling her every demand.

"Scoot forward. Ass to the edge of the counter."

When Roxanne does as requested, I pull her hands in front of her thrusting chest, secure them with my belt, then raise them above her head. Since she's as tiny as a fairy, the bumps in her spine are stretched to their limits when I secure the loose end of my belt around the dual light shade perched above the vanity mirrors.

I grab at my dick while taking a step back to admire the view. The change-up in position means Roxanne's tits sit high on her chest. Even nursing our son hasn't weakened their sultriness. The symmetry between her tits and hips are perfect. Meaty enough to grip but small enough gravity won't take hold for years to come—if ever.

"I don't know what to devour first. Your candy-flavored mouth or your cunt that's so fucking hungry for my attention, it's sucking at your panties." Precum leaks into my trunks when a brilliant idea pops into my head. "Perhaps I should have both."

Disappointment isn't something Roxanne displays while being fucked, but I'm fairly confident that's what blisters out of her eyes when I slip her panties to the side before notching a finger inside of her. She isn't pissed I kept the greediness of my stuff to only one finger, she's stunned I haven't fallen to my knees and devoured her cunt for dessert like I do anytime it's in front of me.

Our fuck this afternoon was hard and fast, but it still only occurred after Roxanne rode my face like I was a bull and she only needed to hold on for eight seconds. I need her wet enough to take me without pain, and screaming my name loud enough the frantic calls men in my industry never stop hearing drown out my wish to kill for another twenty-four hours.

Clawing your way back to nothing is already hard, but when you toss in all the shit my father shrouded our name in, I should have drowned years ago. The only reason I've stayed afloat is because the people around me are stronger than the man who tried to hold my head under the water.

It took me a long time to realize that. The delay didn't weaken the truth of it, though. Roxanne, Rocco, Smith, and perhaps even Clover have kept this train on the tracks, and it continues steaming forward at a rate so fast I'm confident Matteo's bid to be the boss of all bosses won't incur a single protest. If it does... you don't want me to answer that, especially not if it shifts the focus off my wife for a second longer than it already has.

Needing to get my head back into game mode, I swivel my index finger around Roxanne's cunt, growling at how it sucks at my finger. "Forever fucking begging."

Roxanne doesn't deny my claims. She knows what happens to people who lie to me, so she'd never be stupid enough to test the theory.

I pump in and out of her slick slit until the sound of her wetness comes close to overtaking her hearty moans, then I withdraw all contact. I was born a prick, I am still a prick, but that isn't what this is about. I want to sample Roxanne's mouth and cunt at the same time, and this is the only way I can achieve that.

Roxanne's deep exhale dries some of her arousal on my knuckles when I pop my index and middle finger into her mouth. I could have kept it to one digit as I did her cunt, but what can I say, I'm a greedy fucker who loves watching my wife gag on my fingers as if they are my cock.

"Oh..." Roxanne murmurs on a moan, not only turned on by how good she tastes, but also moaning in response to my tongue getting in on the action. I swipe it across the lips curled around my fingers before dueling it with hers.

We kiss for several long minutes, biting, licking, and mouth-fucking each other like we don't need air in our lungs to live. Our pace only slows when Roxanne's impatience gets the better of her. After yanking one of her hands out of the restraint that's extra slippery due to the humidity in the bathroom, she slides it into my trousers.

When her thumb rolls over the bead of precum on the top of my shaft, she breathes heavily into my mouth. "I swear you get thicker every time we fuck," she confesses, her strokes quickening when my fingers find their way back to her drenched cunt.

After yanking off her panties, I pound into her pussy with my fingers like my cock is dying to do. While moaning like she's possessed, Roxanne slides the waistband of my trousers over my ass before yanking down my trunks. Once her hand circles my shaft, she pulls her mouth away from mine, desperate to take in the image of my cock sliding in and out of her tiny hand.

I swear she loves stroking me as much as she does watching me do it on her behalf. She's so fucking obsessed with me bringing myself to climax, she's asked me to do it numerous times the past almost four years. She's even sketched me stroking my cock on more than one occasion.

Her drawings are erotic pieces of art I value as much as the alteration of light that forever occurs when she spots my cock. Whether deflating after a recent fuck session or hardening at the thought of her lips wrapping around the tip while showering, she forever stares at my cock like a hungry little minx who hasn't had it inside of her a minimum once a day for the past four years.

Even having Matteo didn't slow us down. We didn't fuck the three weeks she was out of commission, but Roxanne sure as hell did take my dick between her lips as often as possible. Rocco said I should 'cut the poor girl some slack,' unaware that holding Roxanne back is the equivalent of me issuing mercy to someone who hurt her. Not fucking possible. I'm a man not a saint.

Besides, Roxanne doesn't want a man. She wants a bastard, a killer, a man who'd rather slay her than ever see her with anyone but him, and I'm giving her exactly what she wants.

Roxanne smashes her head into the mirror with a moan when I fall to my knees before delving my head between her legs. "Oh, God."

I drag my tongue up her slick cunt before swiveling it around her clit. It's buzzing with so much energy, I'm confident it will only take two tugs of my teeth to send her freefalling over the edge.

"Look at me," I demand, needing her eyes on me.

The reasoning behind her fascination with sketching her mother's exchanges when she was a child made sense the first time I saw the light in her eyes shift. It wasn't as bright as the gleam in her eyes when Matteo was placed on her chest after a thirteen-hour long labor, but it's had me riveted with voyeurism ever since. Except, I don't want to watch the shift in anyone's eyes. I only want to see it in hers—my wife's.

Once Roxanne's eyes lock with mine, I tug at her clit with my teeth. My growl rolls through her clenching cunt as effectively as the shakes wreaking havoc with her body when she's blindsided by an orgasm.

While screaming my name on repeat, her thighs hug my head, but not once does she attempt to yank me away as she did the blonde who kneeled in front of me all those years ago. She'd rather die from sexual exhaustion than ever deprive me of the one thing I crave more than anything.

As my name falls from her mouth on repeat, I eat her like a crazed man. I poke my tongue inside of her, roll it over her clit, and lap up every droplet of her cum before it comes close to coating my chin, and I do it all with her eyes drinking in every move I do.

Only once her orgasm has been stretched from one to two do I stand to my feet. It's no easy feat with how lightheaded I am. I'm not swaying because my trousers are wrapped around my ankles. It's from how fucking bright the gleam in Roxanne's eyes is. They're lit up to the hilt, brighter than any star in the sky, and nothing but my lips and tongue are responsible for their illumination.

After releasing Roxanne's hand that is still restrained with my belt, I nudge my head to the freestanding shower in our master bathroom. It was custom made to ensure I'd face no issues getting my head between my wife's legs any time we shower together, which is almost every day. "Ass in the shower. I need to add to your wetness."

Roxanne purrs like a little kitty when I backhand her greedy cunt to get across my point. She's wet enough to take me now, back to back orgasms leave no doubt to that. But with it being summer and the temperature beyond fucking hot, I don't want the friction buzzing between us to start an out of control wildfire.

I switch on the faucet, but I don't bother twisting it to hot. Within seconds of me commanding for Roxanne to place one of her feet onto the hob in the shower and to grip the showerhead in a firm hold, she'll be grateful for the coolness of the water, because I'm not about to drive home; I'm ready for my second helping.

"Dimi... ah... God... Fuck," Roxanne mutters when I drop to my knees for the second time before forcing her thighs apart with my head. "It's too much. It's *way* too fucking much."

Her screams echo off the tiled walls along with her moans when I work a third orgasm out of her in under thirty seconds. It's not a new record for us, but for back to back orgasms, it very well could be.

After a second long lick up her convulsing cunt, I slowly make my way up her body. I kiss and caress every inch of her ravishing skin on my trek to her mouth, my pace only slowing to that of a turtle when I reach her stomach. As I cup the little pouch that should have announced she was pregnant without the need of a pregnancy test, I raise my eyes to Roxanne's face.

Although she is smiling, her grin is unconvincing that not all the wetness on her cheeks is from the shower. She's crying, but unlike the time she permanently cut her mother out of her life, these tears are happy ones.

"I love you, Dimitri Petretti," she says loud enough for two blocks over to hear. "I love you so fucking much it hurts."

I finish my climb, curl my hand around her face that's so tiny, my palm swamps her cheek, then say, "As do I, Roxanne. As do fucking I."

2

ROXANNE

I wait for the stragglers of the meeting to make their way out of the boardroom before joining Dimitri at his desk. I've lived with Dimitri for over four years, birthed his son, raised his daughter as if she is my own, and am shockingly pregnant with his third child, yet half the men that just filled this space don't know my name.

At the start, I was worried my lack of presence in Dimitri's life would soon see me on the backfoot in *all* aspects of his life—both business and personal.

Dimitri soon showed me otherwise.

My face is not well-known, but I bring far more value to Dimitri's life than the men paid to be at his side. I'm as valuable as Rocco and Smith, and at times, the only person capable of getting through to Dimitri when ghosts of his past resurrect to haunt him.

Today's meeting wasn't a standard meeting filled with

discussions about distributions and asset management. A majority of it was taken up ruminating about a possible takeover bid by a Russian sanction that once held footholds in this area of Florida.

Dimitri's brother, Nikolai, wasn't mentioned during the meeting, but the groove nestled between Dimitri's brows the past two hours reveals who his focus is on. He doesn't want to believe Nikolai is responsible for the increase in Russian activity in Hopeton the past three months, but since they're barely on speaking terms, he can't straight up ask him if that is the case.

Dimitri and Nikolai don't see eye to eye. Despite them sharing the same DNA, they were born to be rivals. It was evident when Nikolai arrived at Hopeton only months after Fien was released from captivity, and it was still evident when he stabbed his knife into the hand of one of Dimitri's men at the Petretti compound where today's meeting was held.

No one comes to our family home anymore. It's a meeting place for friends and family, not men who'd cut Dimitri out of the equation in an instant if it pocketed them more money and they wouldn't be killed for it within a nanosecond of it happening. Dimitri's change-up was solely based on Nikolai's first arrival in Hopeton.

He arrived on the scene the night I forced Dimitri to dominate me by using his jealousy against him. Rocco is always on hand to rile Dimitri, but even he was left stumped by Nikolai's unexpected arrival. I was sprawled over Dimitri's desk, being spanked as I desperately craved when Smith interrupted the fun as he had the night Dimitri claimed my virginity.

I've never been introduced to Nikolai, but it's clear from the footage I've seen of him that he has a lot of similarities to his younger brother. He didn't request permission to speak with Dimitri, he walked in like he owned the place, smirking when he realized what he had interrupted. I was dressed and walked to the door by the time he reached Dimitri's office, but not even the anger pluming out of Dimitri could eradicate the sweet smell of sex lingering in the air. Furthermore, the chemistry that forever bristles between Dimitri and me is too explosive for a touch of anger to overtake it.

It's lucky Nikolai mistook me as one of the women paid to entertain Dimitri's 'guests,' or I could have seen their exchange ending a whole lot worse than it did. Leaving me unsatisfied already fueled Dimitri's wish to kill. The only reason he held back was because Nikolai arrived bearing gifts. It wasn't 'India's head' as many prospectors before Nikolai arrived with in the hope of cashing in the massive bounty Dimitri placed on her head, but it was the next best thing.

The Dvořáks were aware of India's plan to trap Dimitri. They paid the amount Dimitri's father requested when he placed his son's legacy up for auction, so they deserved to face the scalding of Dimitri's wrath.

Shockingly, the burn was delivered by Nikolai.

He came to Hopeton knowing Dimitri was his brother, but he wasn't here to make a claim to an entity he may mistakenly believe he has a right to rule. He wanted the payment Dimitri placed on the table when India begged her father to put a bounty on my head.

She hated the undeniable connection between Dimitri and

me when we were strangers staring at each other like star-crossed lovers in an alleyway, so there was no way in hell she would ever watch it occur up close. She wanted me dead, and her father was more than willing to grant his only daughter's every wish.

First, he funded Eddie's campaign to seek revenge on my 'infidelity,' then he came to the plate for the second time with a bigger bat when even a man as ignorant as Dimitri's father couldn't miss the spark igniting between Dimitri and me.

Since Mr. Dvořák wasn't brought in alive, Nikolai was only entitled to the fifteen-million-dollar payment Dimitri offered to bring the people behind the bounty on my head to justice. Fifteen million is a massive amount to people like Estelle and me, but to Nikolai it barely made an indent into the capital he required to dethrone his father as Dimitri did when his long-range shot had the accuracy of an Olympic marksman.

Dimitri took his father out with a single bullet to the heart. The only time he has gloated about his victory was when he arrived at our room a mere three minutes after Fien had fallen asleep. It was a glorious night full of orgasms, exchanges of power, and passionate words I thought would take years to leak from Dimitri's mouth.

He was raised by a heartless, cold man, yet he still had the ability to love. It made me love him even more, and had me understanding why he kept his word by paying Nikolai the fifteen-million-dollars he had offered.

I was frustrated when Nikolai inexplicitly stated multiple times during their meeting that they'll never be close to friendly, but I agree with Dimitri, he deserved to collect the bounty.

Once he had proof the Dvořáks were funding India's endeavors to derail me, he took them down, brought proof of his victory to the payee, then flew home the same night.

Dimitri thought that would be the last time he'd see him.

He should have known better.

The new generation of Petrettis don't know the words 'back down,' especially when it comes to protecting the people they love. Dimitri is instilling those traits to Matteo, and it appears as if some of his quirks rubbed off on Nikolai as well.

I wasn't in the vicinity when Nikolai stabbed his knife into the hand of one of Dimitri's men a year ago, but from what I've heard from Rocco, Collin deserved it. Dimitri rarely talks about Justine, but I see the guilt in his eyes anytime her name is mentioned.

He had no choice but to leave her when he did. If he hadn't, I would have most likely died, and Dimitri wouldn't have gotten to within a hair's breadth of Fien. His closeness that night rattled India enough, she pulled back on the reins just a little. Her push on the brakes gave Dimitri breathing room, and it also saw me walking out of hospital instead of being wheeled out in a body bag.

To Dimitri, that alone made the sacrifice to his reputation worth it.

Dimitri was given a chance to make the blemish not as noticeable when Justine was placed up for auction by Nikolai's 'supposed' father only weeks after Nikolai's unexpected arrival to Hopeton. At first, Dimitri refused to place himself in the middle of a battle he didn't belong in, but once he realized who was being auctioned, he swiftly changed his mind.

Even more surprising than that was my lack of jealousy.

I had no right to be resentful he was helping to shelter Justine from more harm. He left her at the mercy of his father. He stopped for me.

If that isn't proof of my importance to him, I'll never be able to convince you.

Vladimir Popov was killed when Nikolai raided the compound Justine was held at. Her location was unearthed because Dimitri wore a tracker after 'purchasing' her.

After those thrilling couple of days, life went back to normal... until now.

Dimitri doesn't take kindly to *anyone* sniffing around his turf, much less stupidly trying to set up shop here. If the Russians mentioned are Nikolai's this time around, I don't see Dimitri holding back. Nikolai has his blood, he is his brother no matter how many times they both deny it, but I'm proof blood doesn't make you family. It's how you treat somebody.

Nikolai's panties are in a twist because he's never given Dimitri the chance to tell his side of the story. In all honesty, that isn't solely Nikolai's fault. To expose his flaws, Dimitri would have to expose his family. That isn't something he's willing to do right now. We mean more to him than the world, so he would never place us at risk to gain the approval of another man—even if he shares his blood.

I arrive at Dimitri's side just as Rocco asks, "What is your gut telling you, D? Is it seeking a war or a prolonged hibernation?" He laughs when Dimitri glares at him during the last half of his statement. "What? How am I to know what you're up to these days. You're too busy knocking your girl up, and I'm..."

Dimitri and I aren't the only ones who notice his sudden trail off of words. Smith is right there with us. "Breaking in faces of anyone who dares to look at your girl sideways."

"What..." A *pfft* vibrates Rocco's lips. "No! I'd *never* do such a thing."

He's a woeful liar. His lips are stretched ear to ear and he's rubbing his hands together like it's Christmas eve instead of the Fourth of July weekend.

Eager to get the focus off him, Rocco says a couple of seconds later, "I think you should talk to Nikolai. Man to fucking man."

"I agree," I back up, not only jumping into the conversation but between Dimitri and Rocco before Dimitri can hit him with more than a rueful glare. "He's going to be in town anyway, so why not kill two birds with one stone?"

"He won't be in town," Dimitri barks out, his tone snappy. "Permission has not been granted for him to arrive. He may think he's top dog since he took his father down, but there are rules not even he can break."

"Are you sure about that?" Rocco asks, still grinning. "Because from what I heard, you both broke the rules when you popped bullets into your fathers."

"Nikolai killed Vladimir with a knife," Smith interrupts after checking the laptop balancing on his hand to make sure he's reporting correct information.

When Rocco backhands Smith in the chest, he almost drops his laptop. "A knife to the heart or a bullet through the heart is the same fucking thing."

"It isn't even close to the same thing."

While they argue the semantics of murder, I round Dimitri's desk. My heart thuds in my chest when he pushes away from the battered material so I can slot into my favorite position on his lap, but is left disappointed when I plant my backside on his desk instead. I need his eyes on me so he can see the honesty in them when I say, "You know as well as I do that Nikolai is arriving here sometime this week. Maddox is about to be released from jail—"

"That could have occurred a shit ton earlier if he had accepted Dimitri's offer."

I continue talking as if Rocco never interrupted me. "Justine is his baby sister. She wouldn't miss his release for anything, and Nikolai would never disappoint her like that."

How do I know this? Dimitri went to hell and back to help Claudia, and we're not even related, so I'm confident when I say Nikolai will be making an interstate visit sometime soon.

"There are rules he must follow."

"Rules you'd ignore in an instant if it had a chance of negatively impacting Fien, Matteo or me." I scoot to the edge of his desk before lowering my head so we meet eye to eye. "Nikolai isn't your enemy, Dimi."

When he attempts to talk, I press my finger to his lips. "He wasn't when he bought the Dvořáks to justice for hurting me, and he wasn't when you sent Collin to 'collect' Justine so Nikolai could finish what he started at the Petretti compound. You *are* family, you were just raised to believe differently."

I inch back before placing my hand on the teeniest bump in my stomach. "The same could have happened to our children *if* you hadn't fought for Fien as your father failed to do for Nikolai." Col knew he had birthed a child with Vladimir's wife, yet he still let Nikolai endure horrific abuse at the hands of his enemy. That isn't something a father does. "Talk to him, threaten him if you must, but don't act like this isn't concerning you as much as it is. You're not fooling anyone, Dimitri—not even someone as simple-minded as me."

The tightening of his jaw reveals he doesn't like me speaking down about myself, but if he won't automatically stand up for his family like I know he wants to, I have no choice but to make it seem as if we can't defend ourselves.

More than satisfaction for a job well done pumps through me when Dimitri says a short time later, "I'll talk to him." His confirmation my ruse had the effect I was aiming for isn't responsible for the jitters skating through me. It is what he says next, "*Once* I've taught you what happens to anyone who dares to speak about you with disrespect." After pushing his chair further away from his desk, he nudges his head to the floor. "On your knees, Roxanne. If my cum can't wash the dirty words out of your mouth, I'm sure my cock can ram them so far down your throat you'll never speak them again without thinking about me first."

I don't need to peer over my shoulder to know Rocco and Smith have left. The swivel of Dimitri's hand when he wordlessly demanded for them to leave is indication enough, not to mention his tattooed hands moving for the belt on his trousers.

A killer is on the warpath and there's only one name on his list.

His wife.

I'd be lying if I said I wasn't tickled pink by the knowledge.

3

DIMITRI

"**A**m I keeping you from something?" I ask Rocco, acting oblivious to where his thoughts have been lately. "Or should I say *someone?*"

While I slip out of the room I share with Roxanne, Rocco grumbles a heap of curse words under his breath. He loves meddling in relationships, but when it includes his, he clams up like he didn't have the gall to kill his father in cold blood.

That was the only time I've ever seen him sweat. I guess it's understandable. You don't feel remorse when you're taking out the trash.

Eager to get things moving so I can get back to my family before they wake, I shift our conversation from personal to business. "Is Nikolai's flight on time?"

Rocco lifts his chin. "To the minute. His pilot is almost as anal as Landon."

His reply makes me smile. Not because Nikolai *believes* his sneak into my town in the wee hours of the morning will go unnoticed, but because I almost have all the Walsh's on payroll. It's amazing what money can achieve. It truly seems as if the world wouldn't spin without it.

After scrubbing my hand across the bristles on my chin, I get back to the task at hand. "Remind Roxanne to take her iron tablet when she wakes. Ollie said her levels are a little low."

"Oh... so a lack of iron is the reason for the circles under her eyes? I thought that was because she was up being thoroughly fucked all night. My bad." He pauses, purses his lips, then asks, "Do you want me to hit Ollie up for some Viagra for you? I've got no shame. I can get the shit you're too embarrassed to ask for but need."

When I shoot him a warning look, he laughs as if I'm not about to gut him where he stands, but mercifully, he also keeps his mouth shut. It's for the best. I may have killed him if he didn't. I'm still a jealous, neurotic prick when it comes to Roxanne, and even with news of Rocco having his own permanent squeeze circulating amongst the crew, I can't rein in my somewhat infuriating neurosis.

"Remind Roxanne about her vitamins, then stay the fuck out of her room unless she needs you." I'd rather stay and take care of business myself, but since that isn't an option, Rocco is the next best thing. He riles me like I won't slit his fucking throat, but my kids think the sun shines out of his ass and he loves them just as much, so he's the second best man for the job.

Does the knowledge make it any easier to walk away? No, it doesn't. But I'd prefer to be gone for an hour or two than not see my wife and kids for months on end like I did Fien. Rocco's presence guarantees that will never happen. He'd slay a thousand men before he'd let anyone hurt my family, and I'd be right there beside him killing the rest.

After handing Rocco the key that opens every room in my home without a hint of disdain on my face, I make my way down the corridor. Unlike my father, I never leave without saying goodbye to my family first. I'll never let anyone take them from me, but if I were to be taken I want them to know they're on my mind when I wake, and the last people in my thoughts before I go to sleep.

Fien is almost six, has two wobbly front teeth, a face of an angel, and almost dead-straight hair, but she is as lax on personal safety as it comes. She doesn't notice me sneaking into her room. I guess to her it's as customary as Roxanne's nightly shouts. I snuck into her room multiple times per night when she was first returned to me, and even now, four years later, I still do it at least twice a night. I get a great amount of satisfaction knowing she's sleeping in her bed, under my roof, unharmed and safe.

After ruffling Fien's hair and kissing her temple, I head for her brother's room next door. Although Matteo's hair is as dark as Fien's and his eyes are just as blue, his personality is on the opposite end of the scale. He's three going on twenty-three, has chompers that cause significant damage any time Rocco pisses him off, and he not only senses my approach when I sneak toward his bed, he springs off his mattress, jabs me in the Adam's apple, then wraps his arms around my neck.

He isn't cuddling me goodbye.

He's showing me he has the strength to choke me out if I was a real intruder.

"*Pew-pew*. Die, dada, die," he stutters through a mouth full of spit and sleepy, drooped lips. "I tilled you."

"Killed. You *killed* me," I correct, aware he hasn't got a grasp on his K words yet. "And good job. You hit my jugular before I had time to respond. I almost swallowed my Adam's apple."

My praise means nothing to most, but to my son, it is as if I lassoed the moon for him.

"Where are you going?" Matteo asks while rubbing a hand over his tired eyes which aren't hazy enough for him not to recognize I'm dressed in my 'work' clothes. "Can I come?"

"Not this time, buddy." I scoop him off my neck before folding down the bedding and placing him back into bed.

I'm a hard ass gangster, but even I can admit his dropped lip cuts through me like a knife. He wants to be a part of the industry he was born to rule so badly he's willing to pretend he is older than he is just on the hope I'll give him a chance to prove himself.

"But I promise you can soon, okay?" I tuck him in before pushing his almost black hair out of his eyes. "But for now, I need you here taking care of mama and sissy for me. We can't let anything happen to them, can we?"

He shakes his head. "And, and, and." He stutters when he's excited. "Not baby brother, either." The 'baby brother' part of his comment clears away half the spit in his mouth.

After wiping his saliva from my face, I arch a brow. "Do you think mommy is having a boy?"

"Uh-huh," he answers without delay, proving what I've always known. He is like me in every way. I also believe Roxanne is having a boy. My belief is so firm, I already have the perfect name picked out for him. "Fien will be angry." Matteo screws up his face before roaring like a bear, replicating his sister's angry face to perfection.

"Sissy won't be mad. If she is, we might have to tickle her into submission."

When I hold out my hands in preparation to tickle him until he pees his pants, he screams blue murder. He hates being tickled. I don't blame him. It's the most emasculating thing in the world. He may only be three, but even he doesn't want his reputation ruined by his father's unkosher parenting.

"All right, all right, calm down," I say when his screams ramp up to a level that would wake the dead. "I'll save my tickles for Fien."

Matteo wipes at his sweaty brow before plopping his backside onto his bed. "Phew, 'cause I need to go potty."

When he charges for the attached bathroom, I spot a stalker I'm stunned he missed. Usually, not a mountain full of candy steals his devotion from his mother when she's in the room.

"Let me guess. You threatened to tickle him, didn't you?" Roxanne saunters into the room, her hips swinging more when she notices my thirsty watch. When my half-smirk answers her question on my behalf, she pulls my hands away from my body, then slips onto my lap.

"Don't fucking tempt me," I growl under my breath when she moans about the reaction my body had to her seductive walk. "Our son is in the bathroom most likely peeing all over the seat, and our daughter is asleep in the room next to us. I don't have the time nor the privacy needed to work through all your kinks."

Roxanne smiles during the first half of my statement, coos at the second, then straight-up pouts throughout the ending. "I didn't come here to tease you." The whine her words are delivered with reveals she's lying. Alas, her wish for me to see sense through the madness is stronger than praying our son falls asleep in the bathroom. "I just wanted to remind you to look at Nikolai like Fien did Matteo when he was born. The connection is there somewhere." She holds her hand over my heart. "It's just buried really, really, *really* deep."

"Deep enough to ever find?" I ask before I can stop myself.

My kids have made me weak.

My wife has made me weak.

But I still wouldn't change one goddamn thing about my life.

Roxanne cups my jaw like she did while reminding me I'm not fighting alone before nodding. "If you're willing to dig deep enough, you'll eventually find it."

Stealing my chance to reply, she presses her lips to mine. The wish for a murderous bloodbath skates through my veins when she fails to open her mouth at the demand of my lashing tongue. I get why she's holding back, I can feel Matteo's beady eyes all the way from the bathroom. I just fucking hate that she's holding back.

Her lips bring me back from the brink. They could very well be the only thing that will see me coming out of today without the blood of my brother on the sleeve of my dress shirt, so I'm not willing to give them up for anything.

"Matteo, close your eyes."

Like the good foot solider he's endeavoring to become, he

snaps his eyes shut in an instant. Always one step ahead of his competitors, he doubles his assurance he can follow orders by clamping his hands over his eyes, and even quicker than that, I ram my tongue down his mother's throat, then kiss her with everything I have.

It isn't the brightest idea I've ever had. Now I have to work out how to exit Matteo's room without him spotting the tent I'm pitching in my pants, but I'd do it all again in an instant if it gives me the same calm, nurturing effect. My life isn't anything close to pretty, but Roxanne's lips on mine remind me that even the most hideous paintings can be seen as artistic when viewed by the right set of eyes.

"Don't shower until I'm home," I murmur against Roxanne's lips after reluctantly pulling back. "Your candy mouth fills my lungs with air, but the greedy sucks of your cunt make breathing an unnecessary requirement."

It dawns on me little ears are listening when Matteo giggles about me saying the word 'cunt.' He has no clue what it means. He merely knows it's a word he isn't allowed to say until he's much, *much* older.

After a final bite of Roxanne's kiss swollen lips, I stand to my feet with her in my arms. I place her onto Matteo's bed, then swing my eyes to my son standing in the doorway of his bathroom with his eyes still clamped. "You're the man of the house now, Matteo. Make sure you take good care of Mama and Sissy until I get back." I do three big strides to the door before stopping and arching back. "And if Uncle Rocco gets into too much mischief, take care of him as well."

Matteo's grin reveals he looks forward to riling Rocco as much as Rocco enjoys riling me. "I will, Dada."

As he bounds across the room to update his mother on all the things he plans to do today, I exit his room. My shoulders grow heavier with every step I take. Confrontations don't faze me, but keeping my family hidden is a challenge I'm slowly growing weary of. I renege on my decision almost every month. The only reason I've stuck to my guns so far is recalling the boot-size bruise on Roxanne's hip four years ago. I failed her back then. She was hurt on my watch, so you can put money on it that I'll do everything in my power to ensure it doesn't happen again.

4

DIMITRI

W ith the hour early, I make it to the Walsh residence
before Nikolai. The two-story home is one of the best
in the street, but it's nothing close to the sprawling mansion I
collected Justine from for our first date. Either the Walsh children are scroogie with their money, or their parents refuse to
accept donations from their offspring. Whatever it is, they're
living well below their means.

I'd dig a little deeper into their financials if I weren't aware
somebody else already has. The ownership in Nikolai's eyes
when he rocked up unannounced last year revealed he'd go to
the end of the earth for Justine, so buying her family estate for
double the asking price seemed like the next logical step.

I invested well when I bought stakes in the Walsh entity,
and no, I'm not solely referring to their beachside mansion
either. Landon was still sour about his first tussle with a Mafia

Prince when I rocked up at his place of employment a month after Nikolai left town for the second time. He didn't make it out of that exchange the same man.

"Has Nikolai arrived yet?" I ask Smith while skimming past the hedges lining one side of the Walsh's rented home.

I doubt the family dog will bark. Smith sent a crew here early this morning in preparation for my arrival. I still get my hands dirty when it comes to *all* aspects of my businesses— excluding whores. Not only am I disinterested in them, Roxanne would gut them where they stood if they stupidly thought they had the chance to come between us—but I now leave the fiddly shit to my men. The more duties I pass on, the more time I have with my family. Considering I lost almost two years with Fien, you can be assured I've become a master of delegation the past four years.

"Not yet. Didn't you hear? His flight isn't scheduled to land until lunch."

I work my jaw side to side. "If you believe that—"

"I need to find myself a new fucking job," Smith interrupts, laughing. "Nikolai doesn't travel during the day because the devil has never seen a sunrise, meaning—"

"He'll arrive at dawn. Like he always does."

My punishment for Roxanne's rile four years ago lasted well into the wee hours of the morning. We were set to break our record for the longest fuck session when Nikolai stole the thunder. He slit the throat of the man I had on the door, made a second one piss his pants, then walked through my family home like he owned the place.

Our tussle that night wasn't close to pretty.

I don't see this morning's ending any better.

The thirst for a bloodbath dries my mouth when I round the corner of Justine's family's home. I asked Rocco to place my best men on this. He did—*if* you exclude Collin's inclusion.

Roxanne was right three nights ago. I took Collin with me to 'collect' my win in the hope Nikolai would finish what I couldn't. Collin is from my father's debunked crew, and although I am now the leader of that chapter, I can't order his demise. Collin has Petretti blood pulsating through his veins. The lineage is as weak as the ties Megan now has with my family, but enough for me to pass on his killing to a man deserving to claim his life.

Regretfully, Nikolai's focus didn't shift from Justine long enough to realize who her collector was when she was auctioned. He's still a fucking hothead, but just like his little brother, his woman has weakened him. I won't know whether that's a good thing or not until he arrives here this morning.

"Were you given much trouble?"

Clover stops barking orders to crank his neck my way. "Do I ever face trouble?" His Arabian accent is still thick even with him living state side for the past six years. "We have half a dozen men in the basement." The way his lips quirk reveals they're not in the basement via their own choice. "We're watching another six surrounding the perimeter. We could move for them now, but Smith said to hold."

Understanding Smith's objective, I lift my chin. If Nikolai arrives without any men flanking the premise, he'll storm inside instead of arriving onto a battlefield unprepared. The latter is more favorable if I want him to come out of our meeting without a bullet wound.

"Justine's parents?"

Clover's smirk would have you convinced he isn't a hired hitman. "Seemed to appreciate the hamper of goodies you had delivered earlier tonight. All residents are accounted for *and* sleeping."

His reply shouldn't thicken my cock, but it does. The hamper filled to the brim with cheeses, delicatessen meats, and enough alcohol to knock a sailor onto his ass wasn't my idea. That was all compliments of Roxanne. She knows how heavy men sleep when they're bellies are full of alcohol since it was the only time she got a couple of hours of peace when she was a child.

"Send three men in with me. Make sure one of them is Collin." *—What? I can't help but hate the prick—* "The remainder can either keep watch out here or head back to the compound. The choice is theirs."

My jaw tightens when Clover's hand shoots out to stop my entrance into the Walsh residence. "You don't think they should wait it out to see how Nikolai responds?"

"No," I answer without pause for consideration. "Nikolai is entering my turf unannounced and uninvited. It'll do him best to remember he has no right to retaliate."

Stealing his chance to reply, I enter the open door on the back patio before making my way to the basement. It only takes me raking my eyes over the gunless and dickless men huddled in the basement once to discover who the leader of their operation is. He's the only one with bloody wrists from fighting the zip-ties circling them.

While pacing his way, I remove my knife from its pouch on my belt. The dark-haired man doesn't cower when I crouch in front of him with my knife braced in front of me. He's too stunned by me cutting off his restraints to talk. "If you're smart, you'll keep those murderous thoughts inside of your head and come with me."

He rolls his wrists before balling his hands into fists. "If I'm not?"

My vicious smirk should tell him everything he needs to know, but just in case, I slice my thumb across my throat.

Certain he has the picture, I house my knife, then spin away from him. He could stab me in the back with the fire stoke balancing on the far side wall, but I'm not worried.

Only a fool goes straight for the jugular of the King.

A true rival takes down the prongs holding up his reign.

While Nikolai's goon follows me up a set of rickety stairs, Smith advises Nikolai's fleet of vehicles have left a private airstrip on the outskirts of Hopeton. He should arrive within the next couple of minutes, giving me plenty of time to commence my ruse.

After taking a seat in the den housing enough cots for a dozen men, I gesture for Nikolai's man to do the same in the seat across from me. Suspicion makes itself known on his face when my suggestion comes without the removal of any guns of the three men flanking me.

He thought I brought him here to kill him. In reality, I'm testing his value. If he survives Nikolai walking in on us seemingly having a private conversation, I'll know he is more valuable than a standard foot soldier. If he's clutching his bludgeoned throat at my feet within seconds of Nikolai's arrival, I can cross him off Nikolai's top ten.

The rankings of Nikolai's men are worthless to most crews, but to me, it's hard to put a price on it. Knowing someone's priorities far exceeds knowing the digits in their bank accounts, because the sooner you learn where someone stands in some-one's life, the sooner you know their weaknesses.

"Cigar?" I make sure the pricy watch Roxanne gifted me at Christmas is seen while offering the goon a cigar that costs more than most men make a year. Since I have time to kill, I may as well work out where his loyalties lie.

Dark hair falls into the man's even darker eyes when he shakes his head. "You should enjoy it. You won't when Nikolai arrives."

His reply humors me, but not as much as the panic that crosses his face when a familiar Russian accent sounds from down the hall. "Is Dimitri aware of my arrival?"

"Nu-uh," I say to the goon seated across from me when his lips twitch to rat me out. "If you so much as breathe heavier, the little red dot on your chest will make a fucking mess."

Usually, I'd kill him just for ruminating over the idea of ratting me out.

Alas, I've changed since I became a father.

I also don't want to subject Justine's family to more gore than I already have. They had to piece their daughter back together after my father ordered for her to be mauled by a dog trained to kill. They don't need more carnage.

I don't know whether to be amused or frustrated when the clamping of the goon's mouth has me hearing Landon's reply. Landon is one of Justine's older brothers. He acts regal, but his exterior is nowhere near as shiny as his brother who spent the last five years in lock up. "But I'm certain he's aware of Maddox's impending release. His crew's presence in Hopeton has doubled the past month."

It didn't double because Maddox has finally stopped taking it up the ass like I did four years ago. It tripled because my family linage is going gangbusters. I can now say my last name without tasting dirt, and soon it will have the honor Roxanne, Fien, and Matteo deserve it to have.

After scrubbing my jaw to loosen its tightness, I say, "For a man who flies all over the world, your geographical knowledge is shit."

As Nikolai's eyes snap to mine, his hand slips into the back pocket of his jeans. Unlike me, who favors guns over knifes, Nikolai is never without his trusty knife. It killed his father, gave him his throne, and awarded him his queen. His favoritism is understandable.

I love carnage. For years, it kept the blood pumping through my veins as black as my son's hair. Now, the cravings are nowhere near as severe. That doesn't mean I won't sit back and watch the occasional massacre occur, though.

Nikolai isn't reaching for his knife solely because I'm in his presence. He spotted Collin standing at my side, and a craving for a bloodbath is seen all over his face.

I'm not the only one noticing it. Clover was a nanosecond from lighting Nikolai's chest up with the scope of his M4. The only reason he didn't is because I signaled for him not to. If Nikolai wants to take out the trash, I'm more than happy to let him.

Disappointment balls my hands when Nikolai doesn't sentence Collin to anything but a murderous glare. I want to say it's because he's weak and pathetic, but I gave up lying around about the same time I took prostitutes off my agenda. Nikolai is holding back because he doesn't want to force Justine to see the vile side of our life any more than I wish I could have kept her off my father's radar. I made mistakes back then, many of them, and only now do I have the chance to make them right.

"Wait for me outside."

My back molars smash together when Collin acts as if I didn't speak. He wrongly believes the Petretti blood in his veins will save him from my wrath. I'm not close to reaching the same conclusion, but before I can show him exactly what happens when you ignore my direct order, Nikolai's goon commences his punishment on my behalf.

He twists Collin's arm around his back before he distorts his neck in a way that isn't close to normal. When he marches him to the door, Clover strays his eyes my way. He's forever on alert. A simple scratch of my nose would see every man in this room taken down in under five seconds, and if the tick in his jaw is anything to go by, Collin would be the first punk-ass on his list.

After taking in a bloody tooth halfway down the hall, smirking when I realize it belongs to Collin, I return my focus to Nikolai. "He's lucky I don't pay him for his looks."

Nikolai tries to ignore the humor in my tone. You can be assured if the mafia kingpin thing doesn't work out for him, he'll never be an actor because his acting skills are shit. "Then what are you paying him for? It can't be his smarts."

While murmuring about the mess my father left me to clean, I shadow Nikolai's walk into the den. He isn't happy I'm here, and the feeling is mutual.

After sitting in the chair his goon just vacated, Nikolai motions from me to sit across from him. I smirk at his gall. It's the least I can do since my hands are itching to creep for my gun. This is *not* his turf, so he doesn't run the show around here.

The smoke from his recently lit cigarette bellows between us when Nikolai says, "You shouldn't be here without an invitation."

I shift on my feet to ensure he can see my face before replying, "I could say the same for you, Nikolai. You don't belong here anymore than I do."

I don't just mean in Hopeton. I mean the throne he's been sitting on the past year. Both our reigns were founded by lies and shady handlings. Only mine is moving out of the shrouds our father cloaked it in.

My thoughts are pulled back to the present when Nikolai discloses, "Justine is with child. *My child.*"

Images of Justine don't roll through my head during his confession. All I can see are the tears in Roxanne's eyes when she demanded for Dr. Klein to scan lower on her abdomen, and the fury that engulfed me when I noticed the boot-size bruise on her hip. It reminds me of how I failed her. How I let my enemies hurt her in a way I swore they never would.

It also has me torn on leaving right now to ensure she never faces that same injustice again and warning Nikolai he should keep quiet about his news. I understand he's proud of his accomplishment, I get he wants to shout his victory from the rooftops, but he could face more than a takeover bid if his enemies discover Justine is carrying the future heir of the Russian cartel.

We were raised by cruel, heartless pricks, but our enemies don't know this since they forever peer at us from below. They stupidly believe we were raised with golden spoons in our mouths, and respect by the bucketloads, so they don't just want us to pay for their inaccurate beliefs, they want us dead for them.

The only way they can do that is by killing the women we love.

I'll never let that happen to Roxanne. I'd kill every person in this godforsaken kingdom before I'd ever let anything happen to her.

As much as this kills me to admit, I believe Nikolai would do the same for Justine.

Mistaking the determination on my face for anarchy, Nikolai asks, "Why are you here?"

I thrust his cockiness back a few notches by replying, "I'm here to issue a warning."

"A warning for what?" His tone reveals his mood is teetering. If it's anything close to the turmoil in my gut, he too will require more than a bloodbath to settle his unease. He'll need the heated cunt of his woman.

I owe this man nothing. He has disrespected me more than I

have *ever* disrespected him, but Roxanne's words before I left this morning are still ringing in my ears. It wasn't by choice, and I'd give anything to change it, but this man is my brother, and I have the DNA evidence to prove it.

With that in mind, I say, "The men Landon mentioned in Hopeton are not my crew. They're a sanction hoping to get a foothold in my area without my approval." When wit flares through Nikolai's eyes, I douse it before it's half lit. "They're Russian."

"Russian?" His voice is as firm as my fists are clenched, but since he doesn't know me, he once again mistakes where my anger stems from. "Why the fuck would I be interested in a two-bit operation with a main focus on sex trafficking? Despite what your daddy told you, there's no money in the prostitution conglomerate."

I take his jab like a man—for the most part. "Rumors are that you're getting soft. That your focus has shifted away from the game."

"Soft?" He all but growls his one word. "The only thing about to get soft is your cock when I cut it off and feed it to you." He lowers his eyes to the gun strapped to my right ankle. "That piece you *think* I'm unaware of wouldn't be there if it weren't for me." He waits for the anger on his face to reach boiling point before adding, "The guns your crew carry when shipping whores between states are marked with my brand. Even the coke your men sniff off their breasts between shipments was purchased from me."

Nikolai stares straight at me, pissed I don't attempt to deny his claims.

Why would I? Guns, whores, and drugs are *all* our businesses are about. If you're not trading in it, you may as well be dead.

Humor raises my lips into my infamous half-smirk when Nikolai snarls, "Disrespect me one more time with claims I'm not running *my* organization to *your* specifications, and we'll soon discover who's soft." He nudges his head to the door his goon marched Collin out of only minutes ago. "This is your final chance to leave before you discover how hard it is to wipe your ass with your non-dominant hand."

What did I tell you? He's a fucking hothead I should be glad to see the back of, but regretfully, I value the opinion of my wife more than worrying about if our exchange will see me as weak.

I demand respect from my men.

I earn it from my wife.

"I came here as a mark of respect..." My words trail off when our conversation is interrupted by the last person I anticipated seeing. Justine is making her way down the stairs, her sturdy footing buckling when she spots my watch. She looks better than the last time I saw her. She's well rested, healthy, and the scars on her shoulders are nowhere near as noticeable since they're sheltered by her long red glossy locks.

Just returning her stare for half a second reminds me of why I left my family under Rocco's watch this morning. I have to make this right. Not just for my family, but for Nikolai's as well.

After returning my eyes to Nikolai, I tell him the real reason for my visit. "Words that should have been spoken years ago never were, resulting in an outcome that will haunt me the rest of my life." I swallow with the hope a bit of spit will lessen the severity of my tone before continuing, "I decided to try a different route today. Don't have me regretting my decision, Nikolai. We may have the same blood pumping through our veins, but we will never be family."

I lock my eyes with Justine to ensure she knows most of my statement was about her. I hate what she went through. I hate that she believes I'm solely responsible for what happened to her, but I'd hate myself even more if I disappointed my wife for the second time. "If it weren't for her, I wouldn't have allowed you within an inch of Hopeton."

While Nikolai moves to protect his queen, I attempt to stop Karma's painful gnaw on my ass. "He has nothing to fear. You may not have paid the debt Col wanted, but you paid more than I wanted you to pay. As far as I'm concerned, you don't owe me anything." Because I am speaking in my native tongue, Nikolai has no clue what I said.

Justine doesn't face the same injustice. She doesn't just understand me, she understands my remorse as well. How do I know this? When she spots Nikolai's sneaky removal of his knife, she shakes her head, wordlessly demanding for him to standdown.

Nikolai doesn't immediately fall into step, and neither does my campaign. "Tell him I am not his enemy."

Sparks of the woman I love are seen in Justine's eyes when she responds, "Tell him yourself." She skirts past me like Roxanne does anytime our arguments get a little hot tempered before moving to Nikolai's side of the den. "He's right here, willing to listen. You just need to speak to him in a language he understands."

I almost laugh at her belief men in this industry listen. The truth has to be drummed into our heads for months before we absorb it, twisted until it suits our beliefs, then redistribute it as if it was part of the plan all along.

"That isn't the way things work in our industry. The only time you become friends with the enemy is when you're planning to take them down." As the words of my wife filter through my head, I say, "He may be the devil's spawn, but he's also my brother. I don't wish him any harm."

Needing to leave before years of hard work is undone in an instant, I dip my chin in farewell before exiting via the front door. Nikolai's men watch me like hawks, but not one of them move for their weapons. I could thank Clover's close shadow for that, but I'm too much of a stubborn prick to do that. They're scared. I can smell it on their skin, see it in their eyes. They know I'm not a man to mess with, and it'll do them best to convince Nikolai the same.

A storm is brewing, but for once, I don't feel the need to grab an umbrella. I can't issue the same guarantee to Nikolai. He's ruling a kingdom he doesn't rightfully own. That alone will have his enemies paying close attention to every move he makes.

How do I know this?

I'm doing the same fucking thing.

Nikolai isn't just my brother. He's my *older* brother, and some would say the true heir to the Petretti entity. I just refuse to hand over the reins without a fight.

My daughter was ripped from my wife's stomach weeks too early, my son was almost killed on the order of my enemy, and my wife was brutalized under my watch.

I faced the carnage head-on.

I lived in hell for years.

So there's no fucking chance I'll ever concede my reign without facing a merciless bloodbath first. This war was founded on lies but it will end with the truth.

5

ROXANNE

I nappropriate thought after inappropriate thought fills my
head when the heavily gruff voice of Dimitri parts the
steam surrounding me. "Eyes to the wall."

He has spent so much time on the field with his men the
past four days, the last time we showered together was the night
I discovered we were expecting again. It's been such a crazy
week, I've hardly had the chance to celebrate the fact we beat
the odds again.

I fell in love with the leader of a cartel entity and lived to
share the ordeal.

I bet there aren't many people who can declare the same.

Our relationship is nothing close to ordinary. We bicker, we
disagree about almost everything, but that's all part and parcel
when you fall in love with a man who was raised to believe love
was only something the weak were blinded by.

Dimitri loves me. Four years ago, I would have never been

game to admit that out loud. Now I face no hesitation whatso-ever. He loves me so much, when I suggest for him to set aside decades of infamy, remorse, and dishonor, he actually stops and considers what I'm saying. For a man who'd prefer to massacre a bus full of tourists over having a conversation it shows great restraint. He wants to be a good man. He was just never shown how to be one.

That's where I come in. And our children. We, *together*, make him a better man.

After leaning into Dimitri's thick and rigid body, I ask on a yawn, "Did you kiss Fien and Matteo goodnight?"

The side effects of this pregnancy are hitting me faster than it did my first. In between organizing catering and transport for a group of women willing to do anything for a bit of cash for an Arabian event this weekend, I napped.

I never nap. The last time I fell asleep in the middle of the day was after I thought I had miscarried Matteo. I'm not just surprised by how tired I've been the past week, I'm also suspi-cious as to what that could mean. I've never been overly good at keeping track of my cycle. I knew of Dimitri's wish to knock me up the instant Matteo was six months old, and I was a virgin before I was thrust into this dark and dangerous world, so I had no reason to be vigilant, but now I'm wondering just how off track I was with my cycle.

I stop trying to recall the last time I could fasten the button in my jeans when Dimitri hums out an agreeing murmur. "Are you aware our son sleeps with a knife under his pillow?"

As I pivot around to face him, I drag my teeth over my lower lip. "Rocco gave it to him. I was supposed to sneak it out once he went to sleep... I kinda forgot."

It's wrong of me to admit I hope he gets angry over my forgetfulness, so I won't. Usually, I seek any excuse for him to dominate me. I can't do that this week. The heavy groove between his brows reveals that would be wrong of me to do. He's struggling, just not all his fight is coming from his brother's side of the field. He hates the distance his enemies continually place between us. We're in his thoughts twenty-four-seven. He just can't stalk us as he has the past four years.

Dimitri wrongly believes cleaning up his father's mess stained his family name more. I'm not close to reaching the same conclusion. He took out the trash and punished those responsible for the mess. That already had his reputation reaching a pinnacle not many men are willing to chip at, so I won't mention the rumors that circulated when his crew massacred over one hundred men and failed to face prosecution for it. It has his enemies convinced he is in favor with Henry Gottle, Snr. the boss of all bosses. He is, but since that's only a small part of his success the past four years, I refuse to give it more credit than it deserves.

Dimitri earned the respect he has. He is feared, revered, and loved. And if my woozy head gets on board with the program, he's about to be adored, too.

The bangs I've yet to grow out fan across my forehead when I take a step back from Dimitri. He's so tall, I have to crank my neck to peer into his eyes so I can watch the light alter in them from me lowering myself onto my knees. I haven't kept my bangs because I'm scared Dimitri will be turned-off by the scar running down one side of my forehead. I don't want to change who I am for anyone. Dimitri loves me the way I am, and I don't give a fuck what anyone else thinks.

As Dimitri gathers my hair behind my head, I nudge him back until he's out of the spray of water. I'm not hogging the water as Dimitri accuses almost every time we shower. I merely don't want anything altering his scrumptious taste.

"This won't free you of punishment for leaving our son unattended with a dangerous weapon—"

I cut him off by swiping my tongue over the slit in the crown of his cock. It weakens his knees in an instant and has his grip on my hair turning deadly. Confident I have him exactly where I want him, I wet my lips before sliding them down his fat shaft. Even now, years after the first time I sucked his dick, my lips still burn from his impressive girth. He has a beautiful cock. Thick, veiny, long, and oh-so-fucking delicious.

Just recalling how scrumptious he tastes has me taking him to the very back of my throat. His cock will never fit all the way in, but the flattening of my tongue and the relaxation of my throat muscles has his dick burrowing out in the very back. I deep throat him like he's not stuffing his cock down my throat to suffocate my moans while licking, sucking, and hollowing my cheeks like we're the only two people in the world.

"If you want to taste my cum, Roxie, you better get a whole heap louder than that. I ain't taking no prisoners today. Your ass is mine until the AM," Dimitri says a couple of pumps later.

While grunting through the humid, almost sickly conditions surrounding us, he doubles the rock of his hips. He feeds his cock in and out of my mouth, my horniness ramping up when he needs to fist his shaft with his spare hand to guide his thrusts. I love watching him stroke his cock. My favorite sketches are the ones of him sprawled across our king-size bed with his cock in his hand and his eyes on me. I feel inanely sexy knowing I turn him on enough he can bring himself to climax even while I'm fully clothed.

"That's it, baby. Take my cock all the way down your throat."

I love it when he calls me 'baby.' It's rare to get a nickname out of him, so I cherish every one as if they're too valuable to put a price tag on.

"Fuck me," he grunts through a growl when my gag vibrates against the crown of his cock. He's stuffing his dick so far down my throat, I have no choice but to gag. "That sound will never grow old. And neither the fuck will my cravings for your cunt."

Before I know what's happening, he plucks me from the floor with a tug on my wrist, hoists me up the tiled wall, then buries his head between my legs. The whack of my head smacking into the tiles is brutal, but it has nothing on the sensation that rips through me when he pokes his tongue inside of me before he grazes his teeth over the hood of my clit.

The speed and skill of his licks exposes he wants me to come right now. He hates being denied my taste even more than I hated seeing the pain in his eyes when he returned from his meet-up with Nikolai days ago. I don't know what was said, Smith denied me access to the footage on Dimitri's orders, but I didn't need to hear the words they exchanged to understand Dimitri's remorse. It was written all over his face.

My thoughts are returned to the present by Dimitri sucking

my clit into his mouth. Basking the bud of nerves between the folds of my pussy with his attention isn't unintentional. He's a master at reading me, an absolute pro. He knew my thoughts had drifted to another man, and he'll spend the next several hours punishing me for my insolence.

I'd be a liar if I said I wasn't pleased by the idea.

Dimitri spreads my thighs wider by stepping closer to me, forcing them apart by the broadness of his shoulders. Once he has me at his complete mercy, he slips two fingers inside of me. I almost jolt into the air when his thumb rubs at my clit. It's rougher than it usually is, calloused by the amount of dirt he's been forced to stain his hands with the past week.

He'd never admit it, but the guilt he feels over what happened to Justine sees him going to the end of the earth to right his wrong. He hasn't done that for anyone but his family the past six years, and the struggle is heard in his clipped tone when he growls, "Goddammit, Roxanne, give me what I fuckin' want."

He bombards my pussy with wet, hard kisses that have me freefalling into ecstasy in an embarrassingly quick eight seconds. I scream his name while tugging on his drenched hair. The harder I pull, the faster he eats me.

When the calls of a woman on the brink of insanity taper, Dimitri grips my ass, then fucks me with his mouth until my orgasm stretches from one to two. It's an almost cruel, somewhat unstable, but also caring exchange that proves what I determined in the alleyway all those years ago. Dimitri is dark and dangerous, but he is everything I could have ever wished for.

I don't want normal, safe, and predictable.

That's boring.

You only get one life, so it'll do you best to make the most of it. If that can't be achieved without an air of danger, then so be it, bring out the arsenal, because I guarantee it will never be as blistering as the energy that forever teems between Dimitri and me.

It's even more explosive when he stands to his feet, grips his cock, lines it up with my pussy, then drives home. I scream like I'm being murdered. We've fucked many times the past four years, but there will never be a day I'll take his cock without pain. He's too thick for that, too lengthy.

It's taking everything I have not to crumble into a blubbering, shuddering imbecile. That's how good he makes me feel. Even with his cock pounding into me like he's possessed, I cherish every pump.

While grunting in my ear about how good it feels to have my heat wrapped around his cock, Dimitri grips my neck firm enough for pleasure to dart down my spine before he thrusts into me over and over again. The jabs he hits my uterus with are painful, but I won't ever stop him. He's using my body to get out his frustrations of the past week. Fucking me pulls him out of the darkness. It brings him back to me, so even if I can't walk for days after this, I'll face the injustice, because knowing I'm all he needs to bring him back from the brink is an even bigger turn on than seeing the light in his eyes alter when they collide with mine.

"There you are," I say to him as he has me numerous times the past four years before cupping his jaw and kissing him with everything I have. I express how proud I am of him with licks, nibs, and a heap of tongue, and that he isn't just the best father, he's also the best husband. He works himself to the bone to take care of us, and that makes me love him even more. "I love you, Dimi."

My words are jutted by the brutal pounds of his cock, but I know they're getting through to him. Not only does the light in his eyes shine so brightly I'm convinced it is almost dawn, he grunts out words I'd go to hell and back to hear time and time again. "As do I, Roxanne. As do I."

6

ROXANNE

My eyes shoot to the door when a tap sounds through it. Dimitri and I are in a tangled mess on our bed. Sweat is drenching my hair even more than the shower we shared, and I'm reasonably sure my outsides are wearing as much cum as my insides. We fucked for hours. It was glorious, but my god am I exhausted. Matteo's sleeping pattern is as bad as his fathers, and Fien hasn't had daytime naps in two years. I should be sleeping, but for the life of me, I can't. It feels like a storm is brewing. I can smell the rain on the horizon. It just feels like more than a downpour is about to occur.

I think Dimitri is sensing the same thing. He isn't usually a cuddler, but I've spent the last twenty minutes with my head on his chest, having my hair raked by his tattooed fingers. That's as foreign as Matteo sleeping past six. Very unlikely. Don't get me wrong, I'm relishing the rare snippet of peace, but it still feels odd.

When Dimitri hands me his shirt, I drag my teeth over my lower lip to hide my ill-timed smile. Every inch of our family home is wired to the hilt with surveillance—*except* our bedroom. Dimitri isn't lying when he says he'd bury me beneath six foot of dirt before he'd ever let anyone see me naked. Although Smith would never snoop, Dimitri is untrusting of everyone's motives. It's a hard neurosis for him to give up since it was drummed into him since birth.

After ensuring my private parts are covered, Dimitri tugs on a pair of jeans before he heads for the door. Like a woman who wasn't already pushed to the brink of ecstasy multiple times tonight, I stalk his walk. He has such an arrogant stride. It sets my pulse racing even more than when I discover who is on the other side of the door.

Rocco loves riling Dimitri, but not even he is so stupid to interrupt us during a marathon sex romp. We've been mauling each other for almost four hours but that doesn't mean we're close to being done. Dimitri has only expelled half the angst making him more reserved than he usually is, so my job is not yet done.

"What is it?" I ask Dimitri when Rocco's departure is quickly followed by Dimitri moving to the walk-in closet to get me some clothes. "Dimitri—"

"I need you to get dressed and come with me."

You have no clue how dry those words make my throat. I haven't heard them for years, but they're like a scar that refuses to heal. They're burned into my heart, meaning I not only stumble while clambering out of bed, I almost cry as well.

My heart thuds against my chest while thrusting my arms

into the jacket Dimitri is holding out for me. It's July, in Florida. It's way too hot for a jacket, not to mention one that's lined with steel plates.

"It's okay, baby," I assure Fien when she's walked into our room by a group of men with guns strapped to their chests. Even with her being the princess of the Italian Cartel, her eyes are wide and full of fear. "Come to Momma."

After weaving my fingers through her dead straight locks to fix the kinks, I assist her into the coat Dimitri had specifically commissioned for his family. They're bulletproof, bomb proof, but nothing close to panic proof. I'm scared out of my mind we're being walked through the procedure Dimitri assured would only ever be a drill. He hasn't handled a takeover bid in years, so why now is he suddenly being hit with one.

Nikolai.

"Is this about Nikolai? Is he coming for our family?" The shock in my tone can't be helped. Dimitri said Justine was pregnant with Nikolai's child, so why didn't the knowledge he's about to become a father soften Nikolai as it did Dimitri.

Furthermore, Dimitri isn't his enemy. He wasn't when he paid him fifteen million dollars for the raid he undertook in Czechia four years ago, and he wasn't the past four days when he worked sun-up to sundown to put rumors to rest a Russian entity was attempting to place footholds in Hopeton.

"Dimitri!" I shout, frustrated he's once again placing me on the sidelines right as the whistle blows. "Tell me what's going on."

Although he doesn't appreciate my clipped tone, he finishes buttoning Matteo's jacket as if my fear has no basis before he shifts on his feet to face me. "The Petrettis aren't facing a takeover bid. Nikolai is."

Relief is the first thing to engulf me. It's quickly shadowed by confusion. "Then why are we being evacuated?"

He gathers Fien into his arms before hovering his spare hand above the curve in my lower back. He doesn't need to guide Matteo out of our room. He takes control, determined to prove to his daddy he has what it takes to be the leader of the Italian Cartel. "We need to leave because the person hoping to topple Nikolai's reign knows too much for me to ever believe you are safe here." He drops his eyes to mine. His big, brooding frame leaves no doubt he will protect his family no matter what, but his eyes are on the opposing side of the field. Nikolai is his family. He just refuses to acknowledge it right now. "I promised to keep you safe, Roxanne. I won't fuck it up a second time."

"You promised to keep your *family* safe, Dimi. That includes Nikolai."

While guiding me through the foyer of our home, he shakes his head. "He explicitly stated we would never be family."

"Because he was raised by a man as unhinged as your father. Besides, if you truly believed what he said, you would have put steps in place long before now to remove him from the agenda. He is alive because you want him to be." After removing Fien from his arms and placing her into the middle SUV in a line of six at the front of our home, I pivot back around to face Dimitri. "But he won't be by the end of tonight if you don't listen to your heart for once instead of your head."

Some may say I'm mad coercing him to go into battle. It could get him hurt, or worse, killed, but knowing his brother was slayed on his turf without him interfering at all would hurt him more. He has a heart, a massive one. He's just never had the chance to showcase it until now.

"Help your brother, then come back to us. We're not going anywhere, Dimi. We will be at the safehouse, awaiting your return."

My heart whacks out a funky melody when he shifts his eyes to Rocco. He only ever seeks his advice when he's unsure which direction to take. That's proof I'm getting through to him.

As always, Rocco has my back. "I agree with Roxie. He spurts out a heap of shit he doesn't mean, and more times than not he's racing ahead at a million miles an hour... *just like you,* but even snakes have hearts. They might be small, and under a whole heap of ugly fucking scales, but they're still there, none-theless."

Dimitri doesn't laugh along with Rocco. He doesn't move, speak, or breathe. He just stares straight into my eyes long enough to see the pride in them before he shifts his focus to Matteo. "You're the man of the house now, Matteo. Mama and Sissy are now your responsibility."

As Matteo's chest swells with smugness, Rocco slaps Dimitri's with the back of his hand, eager for carnage. The shit-eating grin stretched across his face doesn't linger for long. Dimitri barely shakes his head, but it is the equivalent of jabbing a knife into Rocco's ballooned chest. It deflates as quickly as Matteo's ego when it dawns on him who is actually in-charge while Dimitri is gone.

"Protect my castle, Rocco. If it falls, I fall. No fear."

Although Dimitri could say more, he doesn't need to. The

expression on his face is very telling, much less the look he gives me before he completely obliterates his crew's belief that he's a cruel, cold-hearted man. He doesn't farewell me with a peck on the head like he does Matteo and Fien. He kisses the living hell out of me. Tongue, lips, and teeth all get in on the act. It's the most heartfelt embrace we've ever had, and it has his men cheering and his kids clamping their hands over their eyes. They're acting disgusted by our PDA, but their smiles expose an entirely different set of emotions. They know what love is because we show them at every available opportunity.

Please don't take that the wrong way. Our children will never be subjected to the repulsive, disgusting things my father forced me to endure when I was a child, but I will never hide the fact I love their father from them. He is my world, and until they find their own partners willing to go to the end of the earth for them, he is theirs as well.

"Play to play," I breathe against Dimitri's kiss-swollen lips. "Kill to kill."

"And take down any fucker stupid enough to get in my way," he finalizes, smiling. "Rest, Mama Bear, because when I get back, I'm going to pretend you're not already knocked up with my kid."

Acting as if his murmured comment didn't ignite a firecracker low in my stomach, Dimitri bites my lips, runs his tongue across the sting, pivots on his heels, then hotfoots it to his ride. He climbs into the driver's seat, but his ignition remains unfired until I'm bundled into the backseat of a fleet of SUV's and driven away.

He never leaves before us because he doesn't want our last

thoughts of him to be of him walking away from us. You never know when you may see someone for the last time, so forget the arguments, the bitterness, and the hate, and cherish the good times.

Don't dwell on the person you could have become.

Be Dimitri.

Forgive yourself for accepting less than you deserve, but never give up until you have everything you deserve.

He fought the odds. He beat his demons, and now he will help his brother do the same. I have no fear about this because the good takes time, but the bad can make things occur at the speed of light.

My husband is a murderer, a liar, and a thief, but I love him, and at the end of the day, that's all he needs to bring him back to us.

7

DIMITRI

"Jammers are blocking most signals. Even old school isn't cutting it. Hunter is working on a back channel, but I may lose you once you reach Rico's building."

As Smith's fingers hammer his silicone keyboard, I take the street a block out from Rico's building like a bat out of hell. I'm stunned he's living in Ravenshoe, but it makes sense when you realize the ties he has here. Not only was his wife born and raised in this area of Ravenshoe, his sister resides here too. He has ties to the community, and it's greatly benefiting me. Usually, Hunter would hang up the instant Smith reached out to him. Tonight, he granted him access to Ravenshoe's security system without an exchange of favors.

"The security guard on the door has no record," Smith advises just as I reach the west entrance of Rico's building.

"That isn't necessarily a good thing," interrupts a rough,

gruff voice I'm going to assume is Hunter. "Isaac does security checks on all his staff—"

"Except his wife," Smith butts-in, laughing.

Hunter acts as if he never spoke, "So he'd have some type of online record. If he doesn't..." A smirk raises my lips when he finalizes his sentence by making a throat cutting noise.

I throw open my door before moving to the trunk of my car. It is loaded to the hilt with my weapons of choice. "How many men are they facing?"

"An army," Smith answers before adding numbers into the mix. "Around thirty or forty are storming in via the front entrance."

My jaw almost cracks with annoyance. Nikolai has more than enough men to push back with force, but they're not at his disposal right now. Not even I would turn up with four dozen men in tow for a family dinner. "How far out are Nikolai's men?"

Smith breathes heavily down the line. "Five, ten minutes."

"They don't have five minutes." If the noises pumping out of Rico's apartment are anything to go by, they may not even have two. Silencers are a great way to reduce the number of 911 callers contacting the closest precinct, but it has nothing on the wounded cries of fallen men, and the putrid scent of death.

"How many men are there between Nikolai and me?"

I grow impatient when nothing but the frantic taps of keyboards being overworked sound through my earpiece for the next several seconds. Mercifully, Hunter's grizzly timbre soon gobbles it up. "You've got two in the foyer and six in the stairwell. I'm still scanning the faces of the men in the buildings surrounding your location."

Bang, bang. I lessen his count by two by taking out two men hiding in the shadows of the back entrance. They could have been civilians, but even rich businessmen who like to pretend they're alpha males scream like banshees when they trip over deceased bodies while exiting a building. You don't step over them like they're dog shit unless you're in this industry.

Once I have a customized M6 strapped to my back and several guns stuffed down my pants, I close the boot of my car and hotfoot it toward Rico's building. Adrenaline is surging through my veins, just not all of it is compliments to the rush of a raid. I hated handing my family's protection to Rocco. The only reason I did was because I didn't want to disappoint Roxanne. She's so convinced the sun shines out of my ass, even if I were to return with the blood of a hundred men on my shirt tonight, she'll still take my dick between her lips with a ghost-like grin on her gorgeous face.

I don't want to lose that for anything.

Not for money.

Not for reverence.

Not even for my brother.

I am here *solely* for my wife.

"Left or right, Smith?" I ask after breaking through the paned glass door of Rico's building.

I'm pissed I need to get orders from him, he's usually on the ball, but I guess his delay is understandable. We've never played in this playground before. It's all new.

"Left. Three doors down. Security pad code is 3281."

The eerie silence that usually encroaches every takeover bid overtakes Smith's breaths battering my ears when I creep down a hallway lined with bodies. I don't need to check if the first three victims are breathing. It's clear they died a quick, painless death. The fourth man isn't so lucky. He's gripping his shirt like his hands can fix the bullet wounds in his chest.

I try to walk past him. I try to ignore the plea in his eyes, but something stops me. I want to say it's because I'm a good man, but we both know that is a lie. There's something more at play here. I just have no fucking clue what it is.

"Redirect first responders to the back entrance."

While Smith mimics the voice of an officer in need of emergency assistance, I fist the man's collar and drag him toward the exit I just snuck through seconds ago. I prop him up against the back door so he can't be missed by the medics when they arrive before returning to the door locked by an electronic pad.

Just as I lower the handle, Hunter says, "Guard isn't on payroll..." I stop his reply by popping a bullet between the eyes of the man manning the desk before jackknifing to an African American man seated in the chair next to him. I lower my gun from the man's head to his chest when it dawns on me that he's taped to the chair. I also recognize him. He is Nikolai's advisor —the same man who mocked me when I assured him my claims of a takeover weren't fraudulent.

"Go," Roman begs when I ripped the duct tape from his mouth. "I'll take care of everything down here."

I thrust a gun into his chest with more force than needed before snarling, "Your men are still minutes out."

He absorbs the disappointment in my tone without the

slightest bit of disdain crossing his features. He knows he fucked up, so he isn't going to argue about it.

Not having the time nor the care to ensure he knows the full extent of my annoyance, I move through the building in the direction opposite several residents are fleeing from. Roman pulled the fire alarm, not only giving me the perfect cover to climb a flight of stairs unnoticed, but it will also stop the pesky FBI from getting my face on camera.

Pop, pop. Another two men of the unnamed crew feel the burn of my bullets.

When one of the man's brain explodes onto a door hanging by its hinges, a weird noise sounds out of the earpiece lodged in my ear. It seems as if Hunter is swishing his tongue around his mouth, unaccustomed to the gore that comes from this life.

I'm not surprised. Isaac plays the role of a mob boss well, but he's far from being one. He just stood up to the plate at the right time. It amassed him a favor only someone as smart as him could turn into a multiple billion-dollar empire.

It's rare for me to admit I admire someone. I don't face the same issues with Isaac. Just like the digits in my bank account, he is responsible for every one of them in his. There's just one noticeable difference. His businesses are legitimate. Mine are not.

I get my head back into game mode when Smith's voice crackles out of my earpiece. "Thirty p...erps... o... roof..."

"Smith?" I count to three before calling his name again. "Smith."

When nothing but deadly silence sounds from my earpiece for the next several seconds, I curse under my breath, armor up, then race onto the battlefield as if my pregnant wife's only shield of defense is a dining room table upended on its side.

After charging into the cozy, yet understated apartment, I take a few moments to survey the scene. Considering they're outnumbered twenty to one, Nikolai and Rico have remarkably maintained control. That might have something to do with the machine gun Rico is yielding like a real-life motherfucking gangster. He slices the swell of insurgents in half in one fell swoop and will be set to deplete the rest *if* the assailant sneaking up on him doesn't end his campaign.

Since I have the means to ensure that doesn't occur, I put actions into play. The man creeping his way falls back with a thud when I take him down with a direct kill shot between the brows.

The light in his eyes has only just been snuffed when Smith's frantic voice breaks through the shrill of my pulse in my ears. "Get. Out. Now!"

I lock my eyes with Nikolai. The sheer warning in them should tell him everything he needs to know, but in case it doesn't, I add words into the mix. "They're swarming you from all angles. You need to get into the open before they kill you all."

A grunt leaves my lips when my conversation with Nikolai is interrupted by a perp with a machete. He charges at me with his hands held high in the air, leaving his chest exposed to the brutality I was raised by.

I jab my knife into his chest before dragging it down, smiling when shock darts through his eyes a mere second before he falls to his knees. He's stunned I didn't shoot him. I don't have the heart to tell him his life wasn't worth the cost of a bullet.

When a second man comes at me, I swoop down low, slice the tendons on the back of his knees, then pop back up before he knows what hit him.

I'm just as astounded as him when Nikolai shouts, "Take them," a mere second before he thrusts Justine to my side of the room. Just like me, he'd rather side with his enemy than see his woman get hurt.

"Go with Dimitri," he says to Justine after taking down a man to the left of me. "He'll keep you safe."

Justine is shaking like a leaf, but no amount of jitters can hide the bob of her head. She's awarding me a trust I've only ever been given from one woman, and it has my thoughts so far away from the carnage prevailing in front of me, I don't feel the halo of bullets racing my way until one of them shreds through my shoulder.

As images of my wife and children filter through my head, I fall to the ground. My stumble doesn't come without additional carnage. I take down three perps during my collapse before my gallantry is thwarted by a second bullet ripping through my stomach.

While wheezing through the blood creeping up my windpipe, I roll onto my side so the frantic cries of my wife sounding out of my earpiece aren't gobbled up by the chaos I was born to rule but sometimes wish I didn't know. I should have known she'd be listening. She's too stubborn for her own good, and too fucking caring to ever let me believe I'm walking alone.

"H...elp is coming, Dimi. Sm...ith... dispatch... C... Clover... S...s...stay..."

As Roxanne's chopped up confirmation that help is on its way trickles into my ears, I allow the peace floating above me to settle around me. Not enough I'll walk toward the gates of hell anytime soon, but enough I can recall the peaceful expression on Roxanne's face earlier tonight when she was nuzzled in my chest.

I was born craving chaos. I sought it as often as I did a woman to warm my sheets each night, and created it at every available opportunity—*except* tonight. I relished that twenty minutes Roxanne was cradled in my chest so much it was the sole reason I initiated evacuation orders when Smith caught wind of a takeover bid. To ensure my family's safety, I was willing to be seen as a coward. I would have taken it up the ass for as long as my enemies demanded if it guaranteed they wouldn't be harmed.

Now I realize that was wrong of me to do.

Roxanne's past pains are what made her the woman she is today. She loves our children so fiercely because she fought for them with everything she had. Taking away her ability to fight for what she believes in will change her. It will make her bitter like my father, vindictive like my mother, and as evil as the man I once emulated to be.

By hiding her away, I kept her safe as promised, but I also stripped her of who she is.

That's almost as bad as succumbing to the blackness engulfing me, although it's nowhere near as headstrong as my final command. "Hand Roxanne the reigns. This is now her monarch."

For years, women in this industry were seen as worthless. They were disposable, unforgettable, and easily replaceable, then Roxanne was thrust into my life.

She could have destroyed me.

I could have destroyed her.

But together, we created a bedlam not even God himself can control.

She made me stronger, she gave my life purpose, and if she's half the woman I saw in her eyes when she stood across from me with mascara-stained cheeks and goth-loving attire, she'll bring the fury of hell to earth to make sure the last image I have of my kids isn't of them in bulletproof jackets.

8

ROXANNE

My breaths come out with a quiver when the expression on Dimitri's face goes from pained to peaceful. He hasn't spoken a word since he ordered for me to become the monarch of his realm, but I know he's still with me. I can feel it in my bones, sense it in the prickling of the hairs on my arms. If the man I loved were dead, I would know it... *wouldn't I?*

My watering eyes lift from the tablet I'm never without when Dimitri is on the 'job' to Rocco when he says, "Grant me permission to go on field." His eyes are as wet as mine, his lip just as gnawed. "Let me get him out of there, Rox. Come on, they're going to fucking slaughter him if you don't order someone there now."

"It's too late," I reply, shocked I can talk through the despair clutching my throat. We're not just halfway to the safehouse Dimitri bought when I was laid up in a hospital bed fighting for my life, we're over sixty miles from Ravenshoe. "Not even a heli-copter could get us there before they storm in."

I twist the screen of the tablet to face Rocco. It reveals there are armed agents stretched down two blocks. They're about to storm Rico's apartment building even more perversely than the final three dozen men who swarmed in via the rooftop garden. Smith had every floor covered. He hadn't considered them entering from above.

"We've at least got to try." As Rocco's eyes bounce between mine, he adds a plea to the many I see in his eyes. "Do you truly think the feds give a fuck if he dies or not? They don't give a fuck about him. They don't give a fuck about anyone. They'll let him bleed out in the ER just so they can claim they took down Dimitri Petretti."

"Someone in the bureau cares about him."

As confusion crosses Rocco's features, I call Smith's name.

Forever on alert, he replies remarkably fast. "I've called Ellie a dozen times. She isn't answering."

I appreciate his blur of the lines, but we need to go well past a favor to get Dimitri out of this alive and without handcuffs circling his wrists. "Call Isabelle Holt."

Smith exhales a deep breath. "What?" He only spoke one word, but it relays how stupid he thinks I am. "They're not related."

"No, Dimitri and Izzy aren't related. I don't even know if they know one another, but Rico is her brother, and Dimitri was shot protecting him and her sister-in-law."

"That's a stretch, Roxie," Rocco breathes out, jumping back into the conversation. "But it could work."

While Rocco coaches Smith on what to say to Isabelle—if he can get past her husband—I lean over the privacy partition so I can redirect the driver to a secondary location.

"Are you sure this is what Dimitri would want?" asks Preacher, uneased I'm guiding a fleet of pricy vehicles to an area well-known for its love of hotwiring.

"I'm sure," I reply, hopeful I'm not making a mistake.

It's rare for people to get the chance to redeem themselves, so I can only hope my mother doesn't squander the opportunity. If she hurts my babies while I endeavor to safe their father, I'll let Dimitri kill her as he wanted to years ago, and I won't shed a tear while he does it.

The unease twisting in my stomach gets a moment of reprieve when I glance back down at the tablet. Dimitri's reflection is still in the middle of the frame. He isn't alone. A blonde-haired female agent is pushing swatches of material onto his stomach while screaming for a medic.

Seeing Ellie in her element pops a brilliant idea into my head. It will ensure we will never be friends, but if it gets the father of my children out of the carnage alive, I'll accept it.

"Mama loves you, baby boy." Matteo's dark hair tickles my lips when I press them to his temple. He's passed out cold, the hour drive in the car too much for his little body at this late hour.

I wouldn't be here unless I truly believed this is the last place Dimitri's enemies would look for the heir to the Petretti monarch. Dimitri said we were being evacuated from our family home because the crew endeavoring to topple Nikolai's reign knew too much for him to believe we were safe there. If that 'too much' involves our children, I have to take drastic measures to keep them out of harm's way.

This is as drastic as it gets for me. Even with my mother remaining in rehab for over a year, I cut her out of my life. I didn't want my children to question why my relationship with their grandmother was estranged, so I took the cowards way out and buried the truth under a whole heap of dirt. It made it seem as if I were suffocating the past three years, but its grip around my throat isn't close to the painful squeeze my heart is currently facing.

"It's okay, mama," Fien assures when she spots the wetness in my eyes. "I won't let anything happen to him." She snuggles in close to Matteo's side like she'll forever protect him as I'll always protect her. "Girls can be brave too."

My heart melts a little. "They sure can, Fien. You've shown me that more than once." After kissing her head as I did Matteo, I tuck them in tight before exiting my mother's room.

Although she was issued a full pardon from Dimitri, her life isn't anything close to glamourous. Her apartment is two blocks over from the rat-infested pad Estelle and I shared years ago. Bills are piling up on her kitchen counter, and the last time I had Smith hack into her bank account, she only had a few dollars to her name, but in all honesty, her life is still better than it was. She doesn't have to sell her body to fund her husband's drug addiction, she's not beaten when she fails to live up to his unachievable expectations, and her daughter is happy. At the end of the day, the latter is all any parent should ever strive for.

"Preacher will be stationed in the living room—"

"I won't hurt them," my mother promises, stepping closer to me. She looks healthy now. Gone is the gaunt, waif-like woman I saw walk out of rehab three years ago. Replaced with one who looks like she wants to get her life on track, but she doesn't know how. "I never meant to hurt you either, Roxie."

"Now is not the time to re-hatch decade-old conversations."

She pats my arm in an understanding manner. "I understand. I'm sorry."

The soar in my pulse Fien's comment caused nosedives past my toes. I didn't mean to snap at her like my father always did. It just truly isn't the time for this conversation. Last update I was given, Dimitri was being transported to Ravenshoe Private Hospital. Theater is prepped and ready, and thanks to Isaac Holt, Dimitri's name is at the very top of the list. It gives us a few hours to work my plan through the grinder to smooth out any hidden skeletons my panic has me overlooking, but time won't get Dimitri out of the woods. The resilience of his team without its leader is *all* he has to count on.

I really fucking hope I don't let him down.

9

ROXANNE

"**A**re you ready?"

Strands of thick, dark hair fall into my eyes when I bob my head to Rocco's question. I look nothing like me, but the warrior inside of me can't be concealed by a wig, contacts, and an outfit that aged me by a decade without the need for makeup. "I was born ready."

Rocco's smile is the first one I've seen the past thirty-six hours. Dimitri's team haven't stopped since he was admitted to Ravenshoe Private Hospital under a guarded watch. The Bureau believes he is so dangerous, even his thirteen-hour long surgery was viewed by three agents.

In a way, I'm grateful for the Bureau's panic. Their inability to trust means I didn't have to watch proceedings unfold from the outside in. I was a part of Dimitri's operation even with us being miles apart.

I didn't watch him be operated on because I'm a weirdo

who gets her kicks from blood and gore. I did it because he'd know I was watching. You don't have to see someone directly in front of you to know they're there. You can sense them. No one is ever truly alone. You just have to close your eyes, and everyone you've ever loved is right there in front of you.

Rocco thrusts a blueprint of Ravenshoe Private Hospital to my side of the van Smith is commanding. Its quality has improved from the vehicle he had when Dimitri arrived at the prison Claudia was incarcerated at, but its outer shell gives no indication to the value of the equipment hiding inside of it. "Do you want to do a final once over before you head in?"

I shake my head. "It's all in here." I tap my temple to get across my point.

"All right," Rocco replies, a little uneased. "In and out as fast as you can. Henry's men are waiting in the service elevator, so all you need to do is get him *in* the elevator."

I swallow the lump in my throat before nodding again. "In and out. Got it."

Before the nerves in my stomach have the chance to announce their arrival, I lock my eyes with Smith's in the rearview mirror, wordlessly thank him for his assistance before leaning into Rocco's side. Since our embrace has nothing to do with riling Dimitri, it's quick. However, it is also filled with emotion. If I hadn't bestowed Estelle with the title of being my best friend when we were teens, I would have granted it to Rocco years ago. He truly is one of my best friends, and I'd be lost without him.

"Go get our man, Roxie," he whispers in my ear, doubling

the courage surging through my veins. "Bring him home to his babies."

Home. Such a simple word but oh-so-accurate to describe our unique pairing.

"Stop here," I request to Smith. He's far enough back the security guards on the front entrance of the hospital won't see the head of surgery clambering out the back of a rusty old van. It would look mighty suspicious if Dr. Jae rocked up to work in a shit-box when Isaac Holt pays her millions per year to head his privately funded hospital.

When Smith does as requested, I return his stare in the rearview mirror. "I'll meet you at the docks."

He can't guide my steps today. The Bureau left nothing to chance. If Dimitri's team wants to break him out, they have to go against the full force of the Bureau without any radio equipment.

I'm willing.

Are you?

Confident a thirty-four-year-old medical prodigy would have confidence by the bucketloads, I walk straight for the front entrance of the hospital without the slightest wobble to my stride.

It's hard to keep my expression stonewalled when I dash right past security without having my credentials scrutinized. Regretfully, the rookie agents manning the elevator that goes to the floor Dimitri is a patient at aren't as eager to let me slide by. They stop me by gripping the arm I spent two hours rubbing self-tanning lotion into this morning. Dr. Jae 'supposedly' return from a holiday at the Caribbean early for an undisclosed patient. Since there's no way my morning-sickness-primed preg-nancy glow could compete with her beautiful sun-kissed skin, I got inventive. "This floor is off limits to anyone but the surgical team."

"I'm well aware of that." If Smith could hear me now, he'd be rolling his eyes. Dr. Jae's accent is as unique as his, and I did a shit job reenacting it. "I'm the head of surgery, and late for my rounds." I click my fingers at them like they're bellboys and my Chanel bags were just dumped at their feet. "So be a good lad and hit the buzzer, will you."

Knucklehead number two peers at me as if he thinks I'm cute. The man on his left response is nowhere near as friendly. "Identification card and license."

While grumbling how I'll have his badge if one of my patients dies because he delayed my arrival, I hand him the identification he requested. You didn't really think we'd be so stupid not to consider all obstacles we could face before imple-menting our ruse, did you? Even my eyes have Dr. Jae's beau-tiful oval shaping. It's amazing how different someone can look when they learn how to contour.

"Have a pleasant day, Dr..."

I steal his words by snatching Dr. Jae's stolen identification cards out of his hand. I act as if I'm pissed he wasted my time where, in reality, I'm doing everything in my power to stop him from seeing the relief darting through my eyes. Dr. Jae is a knockout. I am not. I was certain our ruse would fail the instant Rocco suggested for me to pretend I am her.

The drawbacks of being popular is showcased in the worst light when I make my way down the corridor of the surgical unit of Ravenshoe Private Hospital. Most people I pass greet me politely, but the instant I reply, their pleasantries switch to suspicion. Even though they don't approach me, I'm confident rumors will circle the water cooler by the end of today that Dr. Jae's Caribbean holiday was a guise for a facelift in Thailand.

"Chop, chop, get to work!" I snap out, preferring they think I'm a bitch than unmask me in front of two men standing guard at a door partway down.

Since the Feds are keeping Dimitri's admission under wraps, I wasn't aware which room was his until now. They may be plain-clothed, but I can sniff out an agent even better than Rocco.

After snatching up a random patient chart from a door halfway down, I increase the length of my strides. Henry Gottle runs his entity like a captain. If I'm one second late, his ship will sail without Dimitri, our children, and me aboard. I can't let that happen. This is my chance to prove to Dimitri he chose right when he spared my life all those years ago.

Our children own his heart, but only I have the key to unlock it.

I thrust Dr. Jae's identification card under the guard's nose when he attempts to stop my entrance into Dimitri's room. "This patient's file shows he had an integral dissection of the bowel during surgery. If we don't immediately operate, he will die."

I have no idea what I just said, and neither do the guards.

Although they're confused, they stand their ground. "We've been instructed not to let the patient out of our sight."

"Who said he was leaving your sight?" I immediately fire back. "You're going to help me get him to theater."

"Don't you have orderlies for that?"

Ignoring nincompoop number one's question, I step between the men whose shoulders sit higher than my head before pushing through Dimitri's door.

I don't know whether I should laugh or cheer for joy when Dimitri's heavily accented voice booms into my ears a nanosecond later. "If you're here to offer me *another* sponge bath, I'm going to tell you what I told the nurse before you. I'm. Not. Fucking. Interested."

He's such a surly bastard. I love that about him.

"Perhaps you should tell them what your wife will do to them if they're caught even suggesting such atrocious things."

Since I'm still in role, I almost burn at the stake when Dimitri's eyes lift from his handcuffed hand to my face. He looks set to siphon the blood from my veins. He isn't angry about my suggestion. It's acknowledging that he has a wife that sees his anger boiling over.

His eyes don't even make it to my face before it dawns on him who I am. He knows my body as intimately as I do his. He'd never mistake it.

After darting his eyes left to right, he barks out, "What do you want?"

"They're here to assist in your transfer to surgery," I answer on behalf of the agents flanking me. "It's a matter of utmost importance. Dr Fien and Matteo are waiting."

While acting as if my last sentence didn't well my eyes with tears, I snatch up the wheelchair at the side of Dimitri's room before nudging my head to the guards. "Quickly. Do you have any idea how much surgical residence make per year? Your delay is bleeding this operation of money. Pens will be scratched to paper when the board members are advised of your tardiness. I don't think the director of the Bureau will appreciate being nagged during election month."

Like two kids being promised a treat for cleaning their room, the agents jump into action. While one moves to unlock Dimitri's handcuffs so we can transfer him from his bed to the wheelchair, the other agents takes command of Dimitri's mode of transport.

He's the one I jab in the leg with a tranquilizer I hid in the pocket of my white doctor's coat. The other is taken care of by Dimitri. He doesn't kill him. He just chokes him until he passes out like Rocco has been teaching Matteo the past four months.

"We need to move now," I say to Dimitri when the removal of his second cuff sees his hands moving to my face instead of the doorknob. "Henry has men waiting in the service elevator."

With nothing but admiration in his eyes, the last thing I anticipate for Dimitri to say is, "I should kill Rocco for letting you do this."

"You should, but you won't." I arch my brow at him. "You handed the reins to me. This ruse was my idea, so if you're going to punish anyone for insolence it will be me."

"Spoken like a true monarch." His last word comes out in a half moan half groan when I shove him into the wheelchair. It's clear he's in pain, but just like Rocco would never give up the chance to rile him, he'd never let a day go by without assuring me he is the alpha macho male I crave. "I can walk."

"No, you can't. You were shot three times."

"In my stomach," Dimitri argues back. "My legs are fucking fine."

This is so very much like us.

We can argue about anything.

It's our thing.

"If your backside so much as moves an inch out of that wheelchair, mister, I'm going to tell Fien what really happened to her goldfish."

Dimitri scoffs. "I overfed it. That isn't criminal."

"It could be in the eyes of our daughter who adored it."

"You don't play fucking fair," Dimitri grumbles under his breath.

I get up in his face before whispering, "Because I was taught by the best." After kissing the tip of his nose, lessening the redness on his face by a couple of shades, I say, "Put these on." I hand him a pair of gloves and a hoodie. Although it's summer, his tattoos are as recognizable as his eyes. I'll never get him down this corridor unnoticed if I don't hide him.

While he does as asked—for once—I do a quick scan of the corridor. It isn't as empty as I would like, but as Dimitri likes to say, everything seems empty when your eyes are only seeking one person.

After taking back up my station behind his wheelchair, I ask, "Ready?"

My mouth mimics the movements his does when he answers, "I was born ready."

With the timer on my watch beeping in warning that I'm

cutting it close to Henry's deadline, I wheel Dimitri through the door of his room before jackknifing to the right.

"Close the door." When I peer down at Dimitri, lost as to why he's impeding our escape, he mutters, "Do you really think we'll make it two feet away from here with two corpses splayed on the floor?"

"They're not dead. We just stunned them a little. Right?" My stomach gurgles during my last word. There's a gleam in his eyes I know all too well. It's only ever there when his itch to kill has been scratched.

While closing his door with more force than needed, I grumble under my breath how I'm going to shove my boot up Rocco's ass. He told me the syringe was filled with a sedative. I would have never jabbed the agent in the leg if I had known it was going to kill him... My inner monologue drowns out when the voice inside my head screams louder than my lie. I would have gassed the entire hospital if it was the only viable option to free Dimitri.

"There she is," Dimitri growls in a gravelly tone. "My mama bear has her claws at the ready."

Needing to continue with our ploy before I kiss the smugness off his face, I return to his side before wheeling him toward the service elevator. Just as predicted, his large burly frame gains many eyes, but for the most part, they're happy to admire him from a distance. Only the occasional nincompoop has the audacity to wiggle their fingers at him as if he's a celebrity.

I mentally jot down their names for future reference. No one is aware Dimitri has a wife and family, but that doesn't mean I'll let their stupidity slide. The tension between

Dimitri and me even while bickering if enough to light the entire east coast, so they can't act like he's single and ready to mingle.

"You scared me," I say partway down, incapable of ignoring the real reason my stomach is a twisted mess of confusion. "I thought I had lost you."

"I know." He doesn't peer at me. He keeps his head low and his eyes at his feet. "But you could never be so lucky to get rid of me that easy." When he lifts his head, his infamous half-smirk has me forgetting I'm in the process of committing a felony. "And if you were, I would have taken you to hell right along with me, because I'd rather save you from Satan's urchins than never see you again."

A normal person would construe his comment as a threat.

Lucky I'm nothing close to ordinary.

Threatening me is the equivalent of him telling me that he loves me.

"What is it?" I ask Dimitri when his smirk is pushed aside for a snarl.

When I stray my eyes in the direction his narrowed gaze is facing, I spot the cause of is annoyance. Detective Ryan Carter is making his way down the corridor. He too has the eye of many admiring watchers, but just like Dimitri, he isn't interested. He has a wife and kids too. He just doesn't need to hide them from his enemies to keep them safe. Although it didn't stop him from getting shot. His unhindered walk has me hopeful Dimitri's recovery will be just as effortless.

Upon spotting my prolonged gawk, Ryan dips his chin in greeting before he passes by me. I don't need to crank my neck to know he's giving me a second look. I can feel it in my bones—as can Dimitri.

He leaps out of his wheelchair like he wasn't shot two nights ago, curls his arm around my chest, then draws me back until my back is flattened against his torso. He doesn't pierce the pointy end of the syringe into my neck like I did the agent only minutes ago, but his threatening growl that he'll poison me with cyanide sounds authentic. It has Ryan's hands raising into the air long before they reach for his gun.

"Toss your gun to the ground."

Although Ryan isn't happy about Dimitri's demand, he plays along. He's standing across from Dimitri's hospital room's now open door, so he's more than aware how far Dimitri is willing to go to escape.

"Now step back."

Dimitri's shouted command is for Ryan, but it's followed by every person in the corridor *but* Ryan. "Dimi—"

"I said step *the fuck* back." His roar excites me more than it scares me. He'd never hurt me. Not in a million years. He merely wants Ryan to think he will.

As Ryan's eyes bounce between my drenched ones and Dimitri's narrowed ones, he takes a step back. He can't help but be a hero because he has no clue I'm not a damsel in distress who needs saving.

He soon learns the truth when I bob down to gather his gun from the floor.

With my stance replicating the one Dimitri has shown me time and time again in our range at our family ranch, I flick off the safety of Ryan's gun, then line up the barrel with his head. I won't shoot him, despite him being on the opposite side of the law to Dimitri and me. Dimitri respects him.

That alone will save his life.

That alone will see him walking away from today with only a bruised ego.

Ryan's red face exposes he is pissed as fuck we played him, and his anger grows when I blow him a kiss before shadowing Dimitri's walk to the elevator at the end of the hall by sauntering backwards. Dimitri's mean scowl has our approach well-guarded, and Ryan's gun is more than capable of handling the back.

"What floor?" Dimitri asks when we make it into the elevator car unscathed.

"Any," I reply loud enough for Detective Carter to hear. "Because they'll never find us once these doors close."

Confirmation Ryan has faced a similar set of circumstances before confronts me when he roars, "Not again!" a mere second after the elevator doors snap shut with Dimitri and me on the other side.

Then, even quicker than that, the panels above our head are pulled out and Dimitri and I are hoisted into the elevator shaft by a group of men dressed head to toe in black.

When the faintest hum of helicopter blades rotating in the distance purrs into his ears, Dimitri shifts his eyes to me. "We play to play. We kill to kill..."

"And we take down any fucker stupid enough to get in our way."

EPILOGUE
DIMITRI

Four months later...

W hen Roxanne's trace of the circle wound in the middle of my stomach continues past the standard three-second embrace, I scoop her hand into mine then lift it to my mouth. I feel her smile more than I see it when my teeth graze the tips of her fingers. She's nuzzled in my chest, enjoying the last of the sun on a day that would usually be cold if we were anywhere but here.

We're not lazing beachside at Hopeton. We're soaking up the sun at Cefalù, a coastal town in Sicily. It was my favorite place to get away to when life became too much before Audrey was abducted. Now it is my favorite place to live.

We've been here since Henry's luxury yacht dropped us off a little over three months ago. The first two weeks of our trip was nowhere near as glamorous as the final two on Henry's chartered yacht.

In case you were wondering, shipping containers aren't solely used to transport stock. People smuggling has been a part of the cartel as long as drug manufacturing and gun distribution. When you need to move between countries unaware, it makes sense to jump onboard one of the massive cargo ships men in my industry use on a monthly basis.

I complain like we slept on cots in damp, wet boxes. That wasn't close to facilities we had at our disposal, but nothing compares to a top-of-the-line yacht, and don't get me started on the sprawling mansion Roxanne and I purchased with cash our first week here. It has everything our family could ever need. Coastal views, numerous bedrooms I plan to fill with heirs, and a one-of-a-kind surveillance system that keeps me up to date on all things happening in Hopeton.

Our flee from the country we were born in doesn't mean we've permanently cut ties with it. We're just taking a breather for a couple of months, letting the dust settle, so to speak, then we will return to our realm bigger, better, and badder than ever.

I had initially planned to run operations from Cefalù until my second son is born in a couple of months' time, but a delivery earlier this week has had me reconsidering my objectives. It wasn't a threat, ransom, or any of those fucked-up things I faced my first two years of parenthood. It was an invitation to a wedding—an invitation from the last person I *ever* anticipated receiving an invitation from.

Nikolai and his *Ahren* survived their takeover bid. It wasn't pretty, and it took Nikolai a couple of months to lick his wounds, but once his scars scabbed over and his woman's wounds healed, he took a step back and looked at the whole picture.

Because of Roxanne's somewhat infuriating nosy-parkering, that picture included me.

We're not anywhere near being civil. We have too much baggage from our past to ever truly let bygones be bygones, but I will admit, inviting me to his wedding lowered my guard by a smidge. Was it enough for me to decline his offer for my conglomerate to have full prostitution distribution rights on both the east and west coast? No, it was not. But it did have me contemplating a change-up I thought would be years away.

I knew from the moment my eyes landed on Roxanne that she was a badass. She dressed how she pleased, cried in the middle of the street like no one was looking, and held a gun to a law enforcement officer's head just to ensure I wouldn't miss seeing our children grow into adults. She has more than proved she has what it takes to be the wife of a cartel leader, and I'm about ready to shout it from the rooftops.

While raking my fingers through Roxanne's glossy locks, a now favorite hobby of mine, I ask like it's no big deal, "Do you want to get your dress here or risk a Black Friday stampede in Vegas when we land?"

Strands of red hair peel off my chest when Roxanne props herself onto her elbows. As our unborn son makes it known with my thigh he isn't happy about being squashed against it, Roxanne's eyes bounce between mine. "You're accepting Niko-lai's invitation?" She's hardly gotten out her first question when a much more dire one stumbles out of her mouth. "And I'm going with you?"

The ghost-like smile she forever wears when taking my dick between her lips would have you convinced our children aren't on the sandy shore mere feet from us, building a sandcastle. It has me hard in an instant and fighting like hell not to take her where she lays.

I'd get inventive beneath the beach towels if she didn't jump up to her feet like she doesn't have six months' worth of baby growing strapped to her front.

"Where are you going?" I ask when she races for the French doors of the master suite. My tone leaves no doubt as to how I had planned for her to pay for my unusual bend of the rules. I want her cunt filled by me anyway I can get it. My fingers. My tongue. My cock. I don't care what she chooses, I just need her to get her ass back here so I can do one of the many wicked thoughts in my head.

The odds of Nikolai and me patching things up fly out the window when Roxanne replies directly to the source demanding her attention. "There's no time for that," she says while staring at my cock. "I need to book flights, pack, and advise Smith that we will need the kids' passports by the end of the week." I'm not surprised she automatically included our children in her plans. If we go, they go. No fear. "Then I have to organize a pet sitter for the animals. Should someone come here, or should we put them in a kennel?"

Since she isn't speaking to me, I don't answer her. It's for the best. If I had replied, I may have missed her mouthing for me to meet her in the bathroom in five minutes. My wife saw her mother in many compromising positions when she was a child but that doesn't mean she wants to subject her to the same thing.

Sailor has worked hard the past four months to show Roxanne she's a changed woman, and I give her another shot to prove her worth by straying my eyes to her instead of the children's nanny to request permission to thoroughly fuck my wife until supper.

We could sneak away for a quickie, but where's the fun in that?

My wife wants to be ravished by a merciless, coldhearted bastard, and I need more than an hour to slip into character.

Bonus Chapter

Nikolai & Justine

In a world of pain, but forever in love!

CHAPTER ONE

NIKOLAI

A lmost two years ago, I told Justine I'd protect her no matter what. I promised to slit the throat of a thousand men before I'd ever let anything happen to her and that I would stop at nothing to ensure she'd never face more pain than she already has.

Today, I'm not fucking close to keeping my promise.

My *Ahren's* brows are beaded with sweat, her face is as red as the blood that drained from the men who bid on her, and her nails have clawed at my hands like they usually do my back when I'm filling her greedy cunt with my cock. Still, instead of reaching for my knife as I have many times the past two years, I'm repeating the words of the man with his head between her legs while fighting like fuck not to slit his throat once he's done what he was brought here to achieve.

He isn't attempting to steal the devotion away from me like Vladimir did multiple times when I was a child. He's not even looking at her mouthwatering slit with the eyes of a man not in fear for his life. He's striving to keep the rod in her back as hard as it's been the past two years, and for her confidence to remain at the level needed to rule her reign without the slightest bend to her spine.

He's helping my queen become a mother and giving the Popov entity two brand new heirs.

"Just a little longer," Dr. Goyette assures Justine while peering at her over her extended stomach that shrunk dramatically only minutes ago. "I've almost got it removed."

Our daughter, Mila, was born without too much fuss. She charged into the world like a stubborn princess ready to rule her monarch almost six minutes ago, and she's been testing out the durability of her lungs ever since.

Our son, who to this day remains unnamed, isn't as eager to join his big sister in the humidicrib on my left. The midwives were already concerned when he flipped to a breech position partway through Mila's delivery, but their fret skyrocketed when every push Justine did caused the monitor strapped to her stomach to sound an alarm.

I was facing an uphill battle to ignore my itch to kill as it was, but the effort tripled when the head midwife announced they needed to bring a doctor in to assist. No female obstetricians are rostered on today, and since Justine went into labor weeks earlier than her due date, her obstetrician isn't just out of state, she's out of the country as well.

I almost told them no, but then I remembered nothing is above me when it comes to protecting her—my *Ahren*, my slice of heaven in a hot and temperamental place. She went to the depths of hell for me, so the least I can do is set aside my wish to kill any man who dares to make her feel less superior to ensure she doesn't endure more pain than necessary.

The urgency of the midwives claims were unearthed when the doctor arrived in under a minute. He eyed me like he knew *all* my secrets when he entered the delivery suite at a private hospital in the middle of Las Vegas, but the shrill of the equipment next to my *Ahren's* bed saw him leaping into action.

He's spent the last few minutes working on removing the cord wrapped around my son's neck, meaning not once has he returned my gawk.

The expression on Justine's face reveals she's in pain, but she is putting on a brave front. She's a fighter through and through. The toughest woman I've ever met.

"There we go," Dr. Goyette announces before he quickly adds a request for Justine to push.

As my queen resurrects from the dark hole her panic pushed her in, she tucks her chin in close to her chest, re-digs her nails into my tattooed hands, then bears down as per the doctor's instructions. I count to ten in her ear, my voice growing huskier the more the fine hairs on her nape bristle. She's been trapped in a fiery hell for hours; I'm confident her body feels as if it's being torn in two, yet she still can't help but respond to my closeness.

It proves I chose well when I picked her over everything after only knowing her for days. Wealth. Infamy. Family. She comes before them all. For years, anything I loved, Vladimir took, but not even he can take Justine from me. Angels are immortal, so when one convinces a fallen angel he's worthy of love despite his many fuck ups, his love for her lasts longer than immortality. He will love her until the day he dies, and he will continue loving her until he regains his wings solely so they can meet again.

"Good, Justine, keep going," encourages an elderly midwife at the doctor's side.

She has a blue blanket at the ready, and oxygen on standby. I don't know if the oxygen tank is for my son or me. I faced horrific abuse in my childhood. I've been stabbed, shot, scalded, and beaten, yet not one thing I've endured has been as gruesome as this. My wife is hurting. Tears are welling in her eyes, and she appears on the verge of collapse, but there's nothing I can do to help her. Not. One. Single. Fucking. Thing.

I'll protect her no matter what. I will have her back as she does mine. I just need to get her and our children out of danger first. "You're so strong, *Ahren*. So fucking strong. You are a queen worthy of her throne, and you'll never want for anything."

When Justine peers up at me with the same adored look she wore when I freed her from Vladimir's clutch with only the slightest carnage, my wish to go on a murderous rampage is immediately set aside. Only she can strip the carnage from my mind with one glance. Only she can break through the evil I was born shrouded in.

With her hand curled around my bristled jaw like my closeness fills her with more strength than the piercing of her nails in the calloused skin covering my hands, she bears down for the final time.

Our son's entrance into the world is silent. He doesn't scream like Mila did, nor does he move. He remains perfectly still—as motionless as my heart.

"What's wrong with him?" I ask anyone listening, my voice a roar.

I've faced takeover bids, killed the man who raised me without any remorse, and slaughtered men in the thousands before I reached my twenty-fifth birthday, but nothing could have prepared me for the turmoil that hits me in the gut when I realize I'm incapable of saving the one thing I want to protect the most.

My children.

"Go, Nikolai," Justine begs when they race our son to the other side of the room.

I command my legs to move, but for some fucking reason, they refuse to budge. His arms are flopped to his sides like Justine's were when she was raced into an operating theater with blood-soaked pants and a white, ashen face. His eyes are shut, and the blue mottling of his skin looks like bruises.

Those facts alone already have my hand creeping toward my knife, so there's no fucking chance in hell I'll hold back the urge to slit the doctor's throat this time around. Especially if my fucked-up childhood has me mistaking the compressions he's doing to my son's chest as him hurting him. It's clear he's fighting for him as I'll forever protect him, but it's rare for a man born in hell to understand not everyone is evil.

I just need to remember that:

The battleline between good and evil runs through the heart of every man.

- Aleksandr Solzhenitsyn

Relief snuffs my desire to go on a murderous rampage when I spot the faintest flutter in my son's neck after only a handful of compressions. It's barely noticeable, but when it's followed by the cries of a warrior clawing his way out of the trenches, it's as satisfying as the heat of Justine's cunt wrapped around my cock.

He fought Satan and won—more than once.

After rubbing off the murky white gunk coating my son's skin, Dr. Goyette says, "The cord compressed his airways enough to limit his oxygen supply, but his vitals are now good. I'll order additional tests, but for now, how about we warm him up with some skin-to-skin contact."

Since the doctor is more barking out orders than making a suggestion, a midwife wraps our son in a blanket before handing him to the midwife who delivered Mila.

The shudders wreaking havoc with Justine's tiny frame soothe when our twins are placed onto her chest. To maintain her modesty, the midwife then drapes a blanket over the three of them. "There you go, Mrs. Popov. Two beautiful healthy babies."

The foreignness of being called Mrs. Popov increases

Justine's grin when she glances down at our children for the very first time. We only got married three weeks ago. Justine wanted to wait until after the twins were born to wed, but I was born into a loveless, fraudulent marriage, so I did everything in my power to ensure my children wouldn't start their lives the same way.

It was an affair much to glamourous for a man with a heart as black as mine, but everyone in attendance enjoyed themselves—even Dimitri, who arrived a week before our nuptials with news of his own to share.

This kills me to admit, but I had no fucking clue Dimitri lived an entirely different life than what his mafia ties led me to believe. He has a wife, two children, and another on the way.

Did discovering the real reason he left Justine to face the wrath of his father alone have me forgetting everything he put Justine through? Not one fucking bit.

Regretfully, I can't say the same for Justine.

Our children were kicking up a storm when Dimitri's daughter unexpectedly placed her hand on Justine's stomach. While looking into eyes identical to Dimitri's in every way, Justine forgave Dimitri. It wasn't the half-pledged forgiveness she offered him months earlier. She fully forgave him, because in an instant, she understood her nightmare had purpose.

Her scars will never entirely disappear; the nicks scarring her heart will last an eternity. However, even if she knew the injustices that would follow her decision years ago, my queen would have still gone on her date with Dimitri because walking through the gates of hell made her the woman she is today.

It also led her straight to me.

"I'm so fucking proud of you, *Ahren*," I mutter over the coo of our children who are taking in the world like they've been here before.

Since she's no longer separated from the brother she spent the last eight months in the womb with, Mila isn't screaming her lungs out. She's wide-eyed and alert, her baby blues studying her mother as closely as I scrutinized her through the two-way mirror at Las Vegas PD.

Even with her hair a mess and sticking to her temples, and her eyes circled with tiredness, Justine is as beautiful now as she was back then, a true angel in every meaning of the word.

And undoubtably just as stubborn.

"I'm not seeing it," Justine mutters, her voice groggy from an excruciating fourteen hours. "Mila suits her name. It's spunky and cute... just like her. But this little guy..." She runs the hand donning a hospital bracelet over our son's almost red hair. "... he doesn't look like *any* of the names on your list. Igor, Oleg, and Timofey are too gaunt, gothic and..."

"Evil?" I fill in when words elude her.

"Perhaps," she answers, confident enough to speak her mind without fear of repercussion. My queen knows her place. Her crown will never slip. "Our son needs a name—"

"That ensures he won't be messed with. It needs to be strong and abrupt," I interrupt, confident I'm on the money. He won't face the hell I did as a child, and the strength of his name will commence his ruling.

"No." As Justine fists my shirt, aware my mind wandered into the bleak existence of my past, she shakes her head. "He has your blood in his veins, Nikolai. He's already strong."

You can't hurt a man's family and not expect to suffer the consequences of your actions, just like you can't stroke your man's ego and not anticipate an equally powerful response.

With a growl warning her not even a thousand men could stop me from kissing her right now, I tilt my mouth toward Justine's. I get within an inch of her hungry, greedy lips when a high squawk from across the room suspends my lips midair.

"Nikolai?" Dr. Goyette twists the top half of his body to face me. "It *is* you."

His eyes, although filled with fear, are nowhere near as panicked as they should be. I've killed men for interrupting me when I'm intimate with my wife. My knife would be making a mess with his jugular right now if he didn't just save my son's life. He also isn't eyeballing my wife like many men do when they realize she's my only weakness. His eyes aren't even on my *Ahren*. They're staring at the foot I almost lost when I was beaten to within an inch of my life like he's aware not all my swagger is compliments to a massive ego.

"You survived?" Even though he's asking a question, he doesn't wait for me to answer him. "How? You were as good as dead."

I was unaware you could hear blood pressure rising until my tilted chin and arched brow doubles the vein working overtime in the doctor's neck. I'm not stalking him in silence so he's unprepared for my attack. I'm drinking in features I swear I've seen before. He couldn't have been at any raid or takeover bid I was a part of—*he'd be dead if he weren't on my side*—so I must have seen him somewhere else.

Somewhere dark and twisted.

Somewhere cold and damp.

Somewhere a devil cut off his wings so he could help an angel uncocooned from hers years later in the very same room.

The last time I saw the man standing in front of me, I was flat on my back, having my fractured ankle set by a student doctor hoping to one day deliver babies.

Justine's wet eyes bounce between the doctor and me when I mutter, "Roman said you came back every day for two weeks." I don't recall much of what happened after having surgery without anesthesia. I drifted in and out of consciousness for almost a month, and my mental stability was on the rocks even longer than that.

Dr. Goyette nods, agreeing with a notion I've struggled to comprehend for over a decade. Roman didn't force him to my side with the brutal tactics most men in our industry use daily. He was there of his own accord.

"Why?" I sound angry. I'm not. Anger is just my go-to emotion when I'm unsure how to process what's happening. Watching my children be born was way fucking more than I could have ever imagined. Now my head feels like it is about to explode.

Dr. Goyette steps closer to me, ensuring his words are only for my ears. The fact he never ratted me out all those years ago reveal he isn't a tattler. He didn't need to prove his loyalty more. "The knife wounds to your stomach and chest were badly infected. You had a fever higher than my thermometer went. I begged Roman to take you to the hospital—"

"I refused," I interrupt when I recall the stubbornness that almost got me killed. I was admitted at a hospital when

Carmichael I'm-going-to-gut-him-alive Fletcher wooed me with false promises and a guarantee of a life without further abuse. I wasn't returning to that level of hell for anything.

The doctor nods again. "Roman moved you not long after that. I guess he was worried I would force your hand." He swallows like he's suddenly worried. "I wasn't. When I arrived at an empty warehouse, I assumed you had..." He stops before he articulates what we both know would have occurred if he hadn't recognized the infection that almost claimed my leg *and* my life.

"Where did you get the medication you gave me?" As stated earlier, my head was so fucked-up after Vladimir's punishment, I lost more than a few days' worth of memories, but I do recall the blissful high that comes from medically certified drugs.

After floating his eyes over the midwife acting as if she's not eavesdropping on our conversation, Dr. Goyette steps closer to Justine's bed. "I *borrowed* supplies from the hospital I was interning at. I didn't think they'd be enough." His smile reveals he's happy to accept the consequences that come from his confession. "Clearly they were."

While nodding like he's giving himself a mental pat on the back, he squeezes my shoulder like Roman always does. I'm anticipating for the pride in his eyes to be quickly replaced with dollar signs, so you can imagine my shock when he shifts his eyes to Justine and our twins, praises my *Ahren* for a job well done, then exits the room without so much as a request for a favor.

It doesn't matter if you are in my industry or not, being in my favor will do you wonders. I can line your pockets with money even quicker than I can fill your brand new penthouse with whores. Your every want will be taken care of by me, so why the fuck isn't Dr. Goyette milking it for all its worth?

I'd be dead if it weren't for him.

My son may have very well died.

I owe him more than a favor.

I owe him *everything*.

Proof Justine knows me better than anyone is exposed when she mumbles, "He didn't help you because he wanted something, Nikolai. He did it out of the goodness of his heart." She waits for my eyes to sling from the door to her before adding, "Don't look at me like that. Every man has a little bit of good in them. Even the men *like you* who have the percentages royally fucked-up."

Ignoring my warning glare that I'll wash out her filthy mouth with my cock if she curses in front of our children again, Justine pokes out her tongue before she directs her focus to the lone midwife still lingering in her room like a bad smell. "What is Dr. Goyette's first name?"

I have no clue where she's going with this, and neither does the midwife. "Toby. Why?"

"Toby," Justine repeats, her tone softer and more nurturing than the midwife.

She works Dr. Goyette's given name through her head a handful of times before she raises her eyes to mine. The sheer admiration projecting from them means there's no fucking chance I'll ever deny her, so I keep my mouth shut when I instantly agree with what she says next, "Toby is a fitting name for a little boy who'll never stop fighting no matter how bad the odds." After lowering her eyes to our children still staring at her in fascination, she adds, "Toby Alexander Elias and Mila Elizabeth Rose. Those are names suitable for the prince and princess of the Russian Mafia. They're perfect in every way." She returns her eyes to mine. The pride in them nearly knocks me on my ass. My queen is on her throne, ruling her empire. "Just like their father."

Dimitri's series is a spin off of both the **_Enigma Series_** and **_Russian Mob Chronicles_**.

If you want to hear updates on the next story in **The Italian Cartel**, be sure to like my Facebook author page. www.facebook.com/authorshandi

Join my READER's group: https://www.facebook.com/groups/1740600836169853/

Rico and Nikolai's stories have already been released, but Trey, Maddox, and Asher's stories will arrive at some point during 2019/2020.

Join my newsletter to remain informed: Subscribepage.com/AuthorShandi

If you enjoyed this book - please leave a review!

ACKNOWLEDGMENTS

There are so many people who deserve a special mention when you finish the painstaking task of writing a new book. The main: my family! This doesn't solely include the sexy-ass man I married twenty+ years ago or my five kiddies. It includes my readers as well. You have followed me throughout this journey as much as my family. You've watched me grow and saw me stumble, but you stuck with me.

For that alone, I will be *forever* grateful.

Then there are people in my community who have my back no matter what. Emilia, my alpha readers, my cousin Tammy who will straight up tell me if my story is shit, and the hundreds of authors who know firsthand how much effort goes into every story produced, much less be brave enough to share it. This industry isn't easy, but my love for it grows everyday.

And last but not at all least: Nikolai and Dimitri. I'm glad you have finally come together. You still have a long way to go, but I can see things changing.

You've always been brothers, but now you are allies. That's stronger than any DNA proof.

Until next time.

Shandi xx

ALSO BY SHANDI BOYES

Perception Series

Saving Noah (Noah & Emily)

Fighting Jacob (Jacob & Lola)

Taming Nick (Nick & Jenni)

Redeeming Slater (Slater and Kylie)

Saving Emily (Noah & Emily - Novella)

Wrapped Up with Rise Up (Perception Novella - should be read after the Bound Series)

Enigma

Enigma (Isaac & Isabelle #1)

Unraveling an Enigma (Isaac & Isabelle #2)

Enigma The Mystery Unmasked (Isaac & Isabelle #3)

Enigma: The Final Chapter (Isaac & Isabelle #4)

Beneath The Secrets (Hugo & Ava #1)

Beneath The Sheets(Hugo & Ava #2)

Spy Thy Neighbor (Hunter & Paige)

The Opposite Effect (Brax & Clara)

I Married a Mob Boss(Rico & Blaire)

Second Shot(Hawke & Gemma)

The Way We Are(Ryan & Savannah #1)

The Way We Were(Ryan & Savannah #2)

Sugar and Spice (Cormack & Harlow)

Lady In Waiting (Regan & Alex #1)

Man in Queue (Regan & Alex #2)

Couple on Hold(Regan & Alex #3)

Enigma: The Wedding (Isaac and Isabelle)

Silent Vigilante (Brandon and Melody #1)

Hushed Guardian (Brandon & Melody #2)

Quiet Protector (Brandon & Melody #3)

Bound Series

Chains (Marcus & Cleo #1)

Links(Marcus & Cleo #2)

Bound(Marcus & Cleo #3)

Restrain(Marcus & Cleo #4)

Psycho (Dexter & ??)

Russian Mob Chronicles

Nikolai: A Mafia Prince Romance (Nikolai & Justine #1)

Nikolai: Taking Back What's Mine (Nikolai & Justine #2)

Nikolai: What's Left of Me(Nikolai & Justine #3)

Nikolai: Mine to Protect(Nikolai & Justine #4)

Asher: My Russian Revenge (Asher & Zariah)

Nikolai: Through the Devil's Eyes(Nikolai & Justine #5)

Trey (Trey & K)

The Italian Cartel

Dimitri

Roxanne

Reign

Maddox

Rocco

RomCom Standalones

Just Playin' (Elvis & Willow)

The Drop Zone (Colby & Jamie)

Ain't Happenin'(Lorenzo & Skylar)

Short Stories

Christmas Trio (Wesley, Andrew & Mallory -- short story)

Falling For A Stranger (Short Story)

K (A Trey Sequel)

Coming Soon

Skitzo

Made in the USA
Monee, IL
04 October 2022

15212994R10072